NARCISSISTIC ABUSE:

A Destination to Devastation and Destruction

I experienced it!

I witnessed it!

I feared it!

MY TRUTH

Veronica Harvin

U.S. Copyright Office Registration: Service Request ID 1-14988065231 (Filed August 27, 2025)

ISBN:

Published by: Columbus Book Publishers

www.columbusbookpublishers.com/

Printed in the United States of America

Legal Disclaimer:

This is a memoir. It is based on my personal experiences, recollections, and opinions. While every effort has been made to present events truthfully, this book reflects my perspective and memories, which may differ from those of others.

Some names and identifying details have been changed or omitted to protect privacy. Any names that do appear are presented in the context of lived experience and are not intended as legal accusations or clinical diagnoses. Terms such as "narcissist," "covert narcissist," and "NPD" are used throughout this book to describe observed patterns of behavior and my personal experiences. They are not intended as formal medical diagnoses.

This book is not intended to harm, defame, or mislead. It is offered solely for the purpose of education, awareness, and healing.

Dedication

This book is dedicated to my grandchildren. My grandchildren are the light that brightens the darkness, the inspiration that brings hope, and the motivation that supports life.

You were not given explanations for what divided our family. I hope one day you will understand. This book speaks Grandma's truth. I love you always and forever.

Acknowledgments

Special thanks to the quiet tools that helped me find clarity in my voice and expression in my words. The story is mine alone; it is my truth. Having guidance to speak was a gift.

Veronica Harvin

Table of Contents

BEFORE YOU EMBARK ON THIS READING JOURNEY, PLEASE KNOW

I did not write this book to hurt people. I wrote it to speak my truth. I wrote it to survive. I wrote it for every woman or man who has ever been erased by the people who were supposed to love and protect her/him.

In this book, I have addressed issues of pain, betrayal, and emotional devastation. I want to pause a moment to address compassion. I feel compassion for the man I married, for our son, and others whose lives have been shaped by narcissism. I understand that people often hurt others because they carry their unhealed wounds. That is not to justify their destructive actions, but it does make them human. I feel compassion for the man I married and my son because I realize they were wounded by forces in their lives that they had no skills or means to control. I feel a deep compassion for the man I married, recognizing now that he never truly learned what it means to love. He is the product of the environment that shaped him and perhaps even a legacy written in his genes.

I feel loving compassion for my beloved son, the baby I carried in my womb. I realize that some of my unhealed wounds became his wounds.

I once believed that I was protecting him, but I now realize I was overshadowing him in ways that caused him pain. A mother's heart holds compassion for both her son and his father. My story reveals what the father and the son feel for that mother.

Glossary

1. COGNITIVE DISSONANCE: A psychological state where a person holds two conflicting beliefs at the same time. In a narcissistic abusive relationship, it occurs when the victim sees the narcissist's harmful behavior, but still believes the narcissist loves and cares.

2. COGNITIVE EMPATHY: The capacity to compendium another person's emotional state or viewpoint. While it allows for insight into others' feelings, it does not evoke an emotional response or connection to their pain.

3. CONTROL: the act of extreme dominance over another person's life. The narcissist induces guilty feelings and withdraws love when another person does not accept or adhere to the narcissist's thoughts and actions.

4. COVERT CAPTIVITY: Living under control and restriction without physical restraint, where fear, manipulation, or dependency create an invisible prison.

5. DECEPTION: The act of causing one to accept as truth what is false. The narcissist makes vague statements, tells partial truths, minimizes facts, tells lies, or withholds information.

6. DEFLECTION: The act of changing the direction of negativity from one person to another. The narcissist attacks or blames another person for the things the narcissist has done.

7. DEVALUATION: The act of reducing or underestimating the worth of another person. The narcissist diminishes, discredits, or demeans a person they once valued.

8. DISCARD: The abrupt ending of a relationship with a person. The narcissist suddenly ends the relationship with a person cruelly and dismissively.

9. EMOTIONAL ATTACHMENT: A strong emotional bond to someone, often tied to love or safety. In narcissistic abusive relationships, this bond can keep victims connected despite the harm.

10. EMOTIONAL DETACHMENT: A survival response where a person disconnects emotionally to protect themselves. It is often seen in victims of long-term narcissistic abuse as a way to avoid further pain.

11. EMOTIONAL EMPATHY: The ability to feel and share another person's emotions. Most narcissists lack emotional empathy, which allows them to harm others without feeling their pain.

12. EXISTENTIAL LONELINESS: A profound feeling of emotional isolation that exists even when other people are physically present. It stems from being unseen, unheard, and

emotionally neglected, especially in narcissistic relationships where connection is only an illusion.

13. FLYING MONKEYS: People who help a narcissist manipulate, spy on, or attack a victim. Flying monkeys believe the narcissist's lies.

14. GASLIGHTING: The act of manipulating a person to doubt feelings and perception. The narcissist strives to make another person seem or feel "crazy," and insists that a behavior or event a person witnessed did not happen.

15. GOLDEN CHILD: The favored child in a narcissistic family, idealized and praised to reflect the narcissist's image, often at the expense of the scapegoated child.

16. HOOVERING: A manipulation tactic used by narcissists to pull a victim back after they have tried to leave or disconnect. The narcissist uses charm, guilt, or promises to change. It is not used out of love, but to regain control.

17. IDEALIZATION: The act of attributing overly positive qualities to another. The narcissist views another person as the "perfect" ideal partner.

18. INTERMITTENT REINFORCEMENT: A tactic where love or kindness is given unpredictably. The narcissist uses this tactic to confuse victims and to keep them hooked and under control.

19. INVALIDATION: The act of denying, dismissing, or rejecting another person's feelings, thoughts, or behaviors. The narcissist strives to make another person feel that emotions are unacceptable, inaccurate, or insignificant.

20. LOVE BOMBING: The emotional act that involves excessive compliments, attention, or affection to control another person. The narcissist bombards a person with impressive gestures of affection, inordinate attention, or lavish gifts to gain power and control over that person.

21. MANIPULATION: The act designed to influence and control another person. The narcissist aims to change the behaviors and perceptions of another person by deceptive and underhanded means.

22. NARCISSISTIC ALLIANCE: When a narcissist and an ally join forces to target, control, or discredit a victim. This alliance often fuels smear campaigns, gaslighting, manipulation, and isolation.

23. NARCISSISTIC ENVY: A toxic resentment of your joy, strength, or peace. The narcissist does not just want what you have; they want you not to have it.

24. NARCISSISTIC INJURY: The narcissist feels emotional pain when the ego is bruised. The smallest slight can feel like a deep betrayal and can trigger narcissistic rage.

25. NARCISSISTIC RAGE: Extreme anger or silent fury triggered by criticism or rejection. The narcissist uses it as a weapon to punish and to control.

26. NARCISSISTIC SPLITTING: A defense mechanism where a person sees others as entirely good or entirely bad, with no middle ground. Narcissists use splitting to idealize and then devalue their victims, creating emotional whiplash.

27. NARCISSISTIC SUPPLY: The attention, admiration, approval, or control a narcissist needs to feed their ego and maintain their sense of importance and power. A narcissist may seek supply through affairs, using the secrecy and betrayal to boost their ego and feel desired.

28. REJECTION: The act of excluding and pushing a person away. The narcissist shows no affection, no empathy, nor feelings for another person.

29. PASSIVE AGGRESSION: A covert form of hostility where a person expresses anger indirectly rather than openly. The narcissist avoids direct conflict but uses sarcasm, procrastination, or subtle acts of defiance to punish or control others.

30. RUMINATION: The repeated replaying of painful events or conversations in your mind.Keeps victims focused on the abuser and delays healing by trapping them in the past.

31. SCAPEGOAT: The person in a narcissistic family or relationship who is blamed, shamed, or targeted to deflect attention from the abuser's behavior. The scapegoat often becomes the emotional dumping ground and is held responsible for the family's problems.

32. SILENT TREATMENT: A passive-aggressive behavior where one person withholds communication as a way to punish another person. The narcissist intentionally ignores or refuses to talk with another person as a form of punishment.

33. SMEAR CAMPAIGN: A manipulative tactic used by narcissists to destroy the victim's reputation by spreading lies, half-truths, and damaging rumors. The narcissist portrays the victim as unstable, abusive, or mentally ill to discredit them and gain sympathy or support from others.

34. STRATEGIC SURVIVAL: A protective way of staying in an abusive relationship with awareness. It involves emotional detachment and careful behavior to avoid triggering the abuser. It is a survival tactic, not denial.

35. THIEVERY: The act of stealing. The narcissist steals money, steals joy, and steals happiness from another person.

36. TRAUMA BOND: A deep emotional attachment formed between a victim and the narcissist through cycles of abuse and intermittent kindness. The victim becomes psychologically and emotionally

dependent on the narcissist, often confusing abuse with love or loyalty.

37. TRIANGULATION: The act of drawing a third person into a conflict between two people. The narcissist vents to a third person about the relationship with a partner.

Introduction

Since publishing my first book, *"Lurking Behind the Mask,"* I have had time to reflect more deeply on the choices I made during that time of intense trauma, excruciating emotional pain, and devastating abandonment.

I was drowning in confusion and disillusionment. Writing that book became the anchor that saved me from drowning in a sea of despair. I wrote that book from a place of survival, not strategy. Though I used fake names, many people still recognized themselves, and some chose to turn their backs on me. Today, I see with clarity why that happened.

I do not regret telling my truth. I regret only that I did not yet have the clarity I hold today. I was raw, unprotected, and trying to make sense of a life I had barely survived. This second book reflects a deeper understanding, not just of narcissism, but of myself. It is written with clarity of my thoughts and my experiences. It is an evolution; it is a survival.

I understand that the term "narcissist" carries clinical weight, and many believe it should only be used with a formal diagnosis.

The individuals I describe in these pages have not been officially diagnosed by a mental health professional. I do not use the term lightly or casually. Over the years, through lived experience, personal study, support groups, and self-reflection, I came to recognize consistent patterns of narcissistic behavior, including gaslighting, manipulation, projection, emotional abandonment, and the cycles of idealization, devaluation, and discard. I use the term "narcissist" not to diagnose, but as a way to name the patterns that defined my emotional reality. Giving it a name gave me clarity, and clarity helped me survive.

This book includes many of the journal entries I have written since completing my first book. Through these pages, I want to show what life looks like when you remain in a toxic, narcissistic relationship. I want to give voice to the silence that so many are forced to endure. The hard truth is this: it does not get better. It is a painful journey that almost inevitably leads to devastation and destruction.

It breaks my heart to know that countless others are living in narcissistic relationships, unaware that there is even a name for the chaos, the agony, the trauma, and the relentless confusion they face each day. I know this life. I have lived it. So I share my story not to accuse or to shame, but to bring awareness to the hidden cost of long-term emotional and psychological abuse.

If people can define what is happening to them, they can begin to protect themselves. If they can recognize the early signs, they can make decisions that might save their lives, not always in a physical sense, but in the emotional and spiritual sense that truly matters.

Living for decades in a narcissistic relationship is like being a once-vibrant plant left in a dark corner without water or light. Over time, you begin to wither. Slowly, you lose your color, your form, and your voice. Eventually, you are discarded, forgotten, and replaced. Your presence no longer seems to matter. That is the quiet devastation of narcissistic abuse.

This book is not written from a place of vengeance. It is written from the fragile, resilient place of survival. I know that some may read this and feel uncomfortable and perhaps even defensive, especially those who see themselves in these pages.

To my son, who will always be my child: I did not write this book to hurt you. I wrote it to find myself. I wrote it to survive what nearly destroyed me. I carry deep sorrow for the ways I failed you, especially in not protecting you from the harm you and I were both enduring. I was too often lost in confusion to shield you. That regret is a weight I carry with me every day. To anyone reading this who knows me: This is not a story of blame. It is a testimony of truth.

A reflection on how pain repeats when left unspoken and how silence, over time, can suffocate the soul. We are all shaped by the damage done to us, but some of us choose to break the cycle, no matter the cost. I do not view the narcissists in my life as villains. I realize they're also carrying their own unhealed wounds, shaped by generational trauma and patterns they may not even be fully aware of. I do not believe they chose this path. I believe they are trapped in it. That does not make the damage they inflict less real.

I share these words not to seek sympathy, but because I believe that truth spoken, even with trembling hands and tear-stained pages, can save lives. Maybe not mine. But perhaps, someone else.

I Am Who I Am

I was born in a small Southern town shaped by tradition, faith, and survival. Raised in the strict household of my grandmother, where I learned discipline through fear and strength by necessity.

I attended a Methodist church every Sunday, holding on to faith through hymns and hope. I was educated in segregated schools where I studied diligently, worked tirelessly, and graduated as the salutatorian of my class. I went on to earn a BA and an MS degree. I became a member of a sorority and believe deeply in sisterhood, tradition, and the strength of community.

I was a devoted schoolteacher for more than thirty years. I taught children in elementary classrooms, alternative programs, and special education. I am a proud mother and an even prouder grandmother. I am a people pleaser, always wanting peace, never wanting conflict. I have serious trust issues, and I can be quite judgmental at times. I am far from perfect, but I am real. I am honest. I am truthful.

I am not the stories they tell about me. I am not the roles they assign to me. I am not the obedient granddaughter. I am not the silenced wife. I am not the failed mother. I am not the unstable woman. I am not the diagnosis whispered behind my back, or the silence that follows my cries.

I am the woman who endured what should have broken her. I am the teacher who tried to give her students guidance, hope, and inspiration. I am the mother who did her best. I am the grandmother who loves deeply. I am deeply human.

I have been misunderstood, misjudged, and mislabeled. Yet, here I stand, a lone warrior fighting a war I did not choose. I no longer hide behind shame or guilt. I no longer feel the need to prove my worth to anyone who cannot see me, cannot hear me, or value me. I am no longer asking for permission to speak. I speak my truth freely and honestly.

I am who I am. Not perfect. Not bitter. Just finally *Free To Be Me.* I am who I am.

Prologue

When you are raised in an abusive household, the dynamics of abuse begin to feel normal. It is easy to become conditioned to being abused because it is the only way of life you know. This sets the stage for you to become a very vulnerable being. As life happens, you are then easy prey for the predators you encounter along your journey through life.

I am not an overly religious person. Yet, I cannot deny the sense that I am being guided by God, or by some force in the Universe to write this book. I never imagined this would be part of my life's journey, yet here I am, with words flowing from places I did not even know existed within me.

It feels like this story isn't mine to hold onto alone. It has been placed in my hands to release into the world. I believe it will find the people who need it most, and when it does, it will open their eyes, name their pain, and remind them that they are not alone.

Narcissistic abuse is prevalent in so many lives. People are suffering and lingering in narcissistic, abusive relationships, unaware of what it is. They endure in these relationships for long terms, never realizing what is happening to them. They develop life-threatening mental and physical ailments or diseases that are the effects of the "disease," stress, and trauma that evolves and revolves in these narcissistic relationships. The pain can grow unbearable, sometimes even lethal. Many are overcome by physical or mental illness, while others make the most tragic choice of all: suicide. The undeniable fact is that narcissistic abuse is a deadly phenomenon.

The relentless pain of narcissistic abuse cannot be expressed in mere words. This abuse is devastation and destruction to your mind, body, and soul. How can anyone truly recover from that? And if recovery is possible, it is a long and grueling journey. For me, there is no recovery. The roots of my pain run too deeply beneath multiple layers of long-term narcissistic abuse. *"I breathe, but I do not feel alive."*

People need to understand that narcissistic individuals walk among us. They exist, and they are deeply disordered. Their way of thinking, feeling, and interpreting life is often in stark contrast to what most consider normal or emotionally healthy.

At the core of narcissism lies unresolved trauma, often rooted in childhood. These individuals never truly recover from that pain. Instead, they spend their lives in a constant state of defense and constructing a false "self" to protect the fragile one hidden beneath.

Everything centers on protecting that image. To preserve the illusion of who they want the world to believe they are, they will manipulate, gaslight, discard, and charm without hesitation. They move through relationships masked by deception, slipping in and out of people's lives, leaving behind confusion, pain, and broken trust. The mask they wear hides not only who they are from others but, perhaps most tragically, from themselves.

I believe I married into a family where narcissistic abuse has been perpetuated for generations. I have seen the devastation and destruction imposed on innocent people by a grandfather, a father, and a son. All three exhibited similar traits and behaviors.

I have four grandsons in this family. My grandsons have been surrounded by people with strong narcissistic traits all their lives. I worry that any one of the four might develop strong narcissistic traits. I suspect that narcissistic traits have been passed down through the bloodline in this family. Several international studies have shown that narcissism can, in part, be inherited through genetics.

"I cannot be silent!" I speak out because the cycle of narcissistic abuse in my family needs to be broken. I believe it has existed for generations. I want to bring awareness to the extensive destruction and devastation that it brings to the lives of multiple human beings. There is something that propels me to tell my story. *"I cannot be silent!"* Writing this manuscript has been a challenge in many ways. I felt guilt. I had reservations. It is not my intent to hurt anyone. It is not my intent to avenge. It is an intent to seek understanding. It is an intent to seek closure. It is an intent to seek recovery. It is an intent to seek peace.

The man I married is a deeply complex individual. I believe he struggles with a personality disorder. I do not say this as a medical diagnosis; I am not a health professional. I say it as a woman who has lived with him, witnessed his behaviors, and experienced the harmful effects of his behaviors for five decades.

I am not sure if he understands the deadly impact his actions and behaviors have on other people. I believe his actions and behaviors appear perfectly normal in the world where he exists. He can cavalierly step over the devastation and destruction he leaves behind and then walk stalwartly forward, seeking a new challenge with no remorse.

I find myself facing a sobering dilemma in my life. *Should I stay or should I leave?* The man I married and I have lived together since we were 24 and 25 years old. It is extremely difficult to walk away from five decades of what you know to enter a new realm that is foreign and unknown. The man I married is all I have ever known. For decades, he has abused me, yet the thought of a life without him still fills me with fear. To live in that tension is profoundly demoralizing.

The man I married vacillates between staying together and separating on any given day. Our decades together have no effect on him. For him, parting is as easy as remaining. I am the weakling who cannot let go. I think the long-term abuse has affected my brain. I am confused by the need to remain linked to this person who is a threat to my well-being. So, for now, I choose to stay. I do not stay for the better. I do not stay for the worst. I simply stay. Perhaps in the tomorrows to come, there might be a better choice for me.

Author's Clarification

Let me be clear: no individual referenced in this book has been formally diagnosed with narcissistic personality disorder (NPD) or any other personality disorder. I am not a licensed mental health professional, and I make no claim to the authority to diagnose anyone.

What I do claim is lived truth. Throughout this book, I refer to the man I married as having NPD. That is not a medical diagnosis, but rather my personal conclusions drawn from decades of direct experience, reflection, and research. For years, I struggled to understand the emotional, psychological, and spiritual harm I was enduring. Through extensive reading and study of narcissistic abuse, I finally found a language that matched the patterns I had lived through.

The behaviors I describe: gaslighting, manipulation, emotional detachment, triangulation, control, cruelty, projection, and denial are consistent with recognized traits of narcissistic personality disorder.

When I say someone "has NPD" or "is a narcissist," I speak not as a clinician, but as a woman who survived those patterns day after day, year after year. I use these terms as a framework for understanding; a mirror to reflect the truth; and a voice to name what was once unspeakable.

This book is not a clinical analysis. It is a memoir; a testimony; a survivor's effort to bring light to dark places. It is not to accuse, but to name the pain and to help others see their own.

Once you come to see the truth of the narcissist in your life and the behaviors that define them, you can never unsee it. It stays with you. It is etched in your memory, your body, and your soul.

Author's Note

<u>To Men Who Suffer in Silence</u>

Though I speak from the voice of a woman who has survived narcissistic abuse, I write with full awareness that many men endure this same devastation. They suffer quietly, invisibly, and too often without support.

The truth is, men are abused, too. They experience emotional, psychological, and sometimes physical abuse. This abuse could be by women or by narcissists who wear the mask of love. When men cry out, they are often met with laughter, disbelief, or silence. They are told to "man up," to stop complaining. They are dismissed, mocked, and left alone in the wreckage of emotional betrayal.

If you are a man reading these pages and feel your truth echoing in my words, this book is for you, too. You are not weak. You are not imagining things. You are not alone.

The world might not believe your pain, but I do.

The Voice of a Victim

I went to church this morning. I sat through the service. I smiled. I stood. I prayed. When it ended, when I stepped outside, when the doors closed behind me, I returned to my car. It was then, at that moment, that my body collapsed under the weight of what I carry.

I sobbed. I do not mean I cried. I mean, my entire body erupted into gut-wrenching, soul-deep sobs. The kind that leaves you breathless, broken, and stunned by the pain that lives inside of you. I sat there, alone, weeping for what had been done to me, for what I had lost, for who I used to be.

That is what the devastation of narcissistic abuse feels like. It is not just emotional pain. It is a kind of soul death. It crushes your spirit. It scrambles your mind. It leaves you lost and alone in a world you no longer recognize. A world you never imagined could exist.

It is not just the loss of a relationship. It is the loss of yourself. You question your worth, your sanity, your very existence. You become haunted not by ghosts, but by the presence of someone who is still alive, still breathing. Someone who has destroyed you from the inside.

You cannot let go. Not because you do not want to, but because it feels like they live inside you. Their voice echoes in your thoughts. Their judgment governs your choices. You wake with them in your mind and drift to sleep still carrying the sting of their cruelty. The most devastating part is this: You know they hate you; still, a part of you clings to the hope that they will turn and see you, really see you, just once. You are held hostage by a love that was never real and a hate that has always been. Your soul is crushed under the weight of invisible cruelty.

You are on a painful journey; the destination is devastation and destruction.

Message To My Narcissistic Abusers

I am a human being.

I am not your puppet.

I am not your tool.

I am not your toy.

I am not your object.

I am not disposable.

I am not replaceable.

I am a human being.

I have thoughts.

I have feelings.

I have worth.

You do not own me.

You never did.

VERONICA HARVIN

A Life of Servitude

I have come to realize that I lived most of my life as a slave. First to my grandmother, and then to the man I married. They were my masters in name, but in power, in control, and in the way they used me for their own needs without care for who I was inside. They never really saw me; they only saw what I could do for them. They did not love me, they ruled me.

They expected my silence, my obedience, and my loyalty, no matter how much it hurt me. I was never allowed to be fully human. I was never deemed worthy of love and never free enough to rest. The heavy burden of serving them, pleasing them, and fearing them took everything from me. I was their loyal and obedient slave. But now, I speak these words aloud, not in shame, but in truth. Truth has become my pathway to liberation.

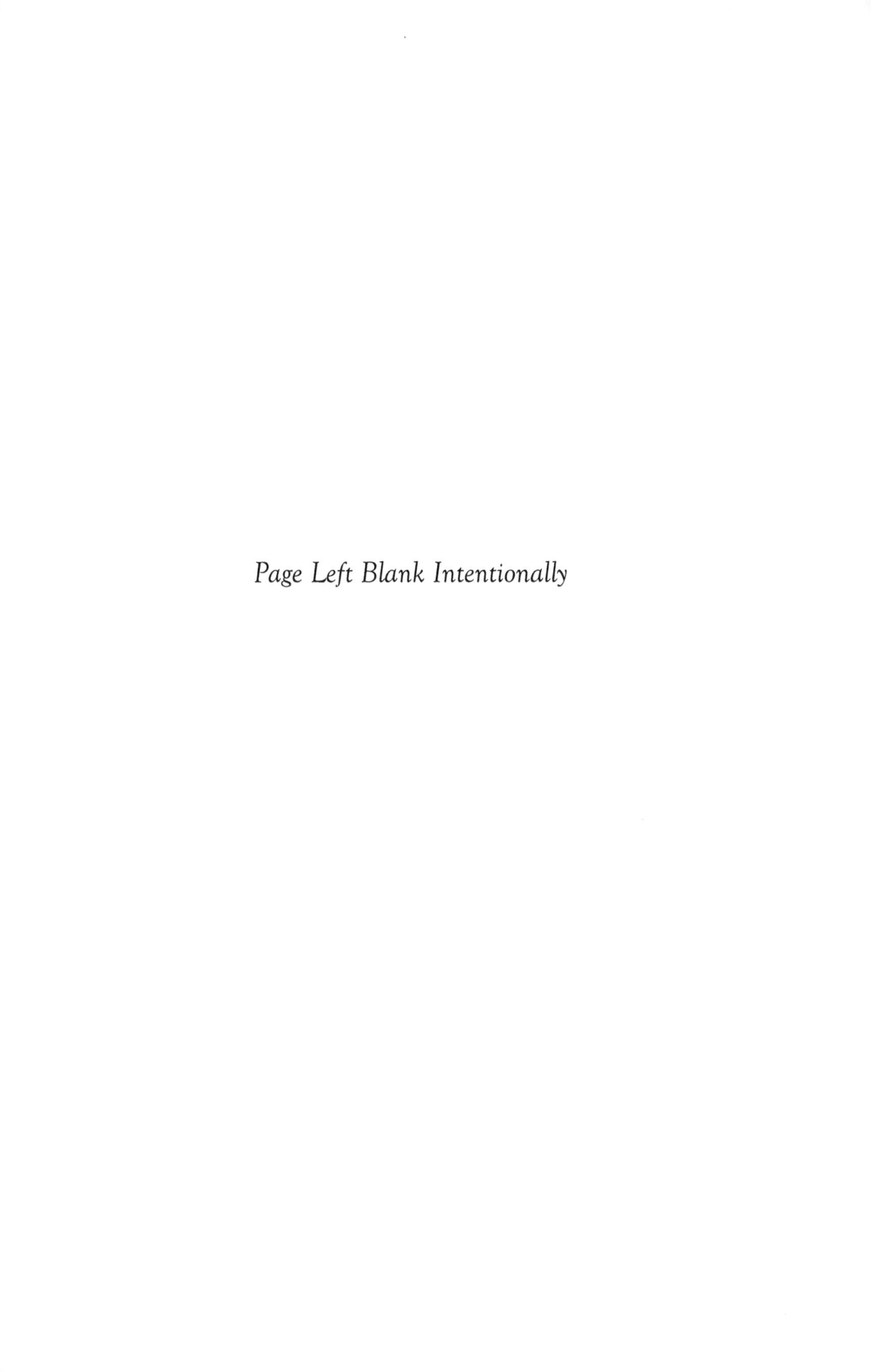

Page Left Blank Intentionally

My Maternal Grandmother

My first slave master was my maternal grandmother. She instilled fear and insecurity that are embedded deep in my soul. She showed no affection and provided no comfort to the wounded child within me. Instead, she was controlling, cold, and distant. Between us, no bond of love existed, only fear that shadowed every moment in her presence.

My grandmother controlled nearly every aspect of my life. The only spaces where I found relief were church and school, my rare sanctuaries of peace and connection. My home was not a place of peace, love, and happiness. My home was a place of anxiety, stress, fear, and constant distress. My maternal grandmother was a formidable and independent woman who raised six children. Her first child was born before she married, and the identity of his father remained a secret she never revealed. In time, my grandmother did marry, but the mystery of that first chapter of her life was never spoken aloud. She and my maternal grandfather had two daughters, my mother and my aunt. Their daughters were teenagers when my grandmother and my grandfather started a new clan. They had three sons.

When the youngest son was still a toddler, my grandfather died suddenly one day en route home while operating a mule and a wagon. My grandmother raised three well-adjusted young men without the presence of their father in their lives. Two of them served their country as US soldiers. They always respected and honored their mother.

Shortly after my maternal grandfather passed away, my grandmother met another man. From what I was told, they were married. I am not entirely sure about that. The new man brought along his teenage son to the family, where there were teenage girls. As often happens, my mother and her new stepbrother formed a connection, and she became pregnant with my brother. In those days, a man was expected to marry the woman he impregnated. So, they got married.

Yes, my mother married her stepbrother. My maternal grandmother married my maternal grandfather, and it is also said that later she married my paternal grandfather.

My father joined the army and went away to fight for our country during World War II. When he returned home from war, he was no longer an active US soldier, but he certainly was an active and virile civilian. During that time, he impregnated my mother and another woman at the same timeframe. My father's other daughter was born in February 1947, and I was born just a month later, in March 1947. I did not know my father very well. I never had any relationship with him. Soon after my birth, my father left town with another woman. This was not the mother of his other daughter. He moved to another state. In doing so, he abandoned a wife and two children, never to return, never to provide support. My father easily abandoned us as if we did not exist and started a new life with another person.

My father's behavior rings narcissistic in my ears. I cannot remember living with my mother at any point in my childhood. I am sure she was devastated by her husband's infidelities, discarding, and abandonment. When I was very young, she left home and moved north. She left my brother and me in the care of our maternal grandmother. My mother came to visit us, and she provided for us from afar. She never came to bring us to live with her. In the end, it was our grandmother who raised us.

My brother was eight years older than I was. I think the age difference was too great for us to establish a close relationship. My only childhood memory is of my grandmother and me. I craved and cried all during my childhood for a mother who was not there.

My grandmother operated a neighborhood grocery store that stood in front of her house. This was very common in the segregated South. My grandmother's store provided food to many people in our neighborhood. Many of us were living at or near the poverty level. I worked in the store from morning until late at night. There were times when I would have to get out of my bed because someone wanted something from the store. I did not stay stationed in the store. Whenever a customer called out, I had to stop whatever I was doing and tend to them.

I would most likely be inside the house, cooking, cleaning, washing, or ironing at any given time. I would cease whatever task I was doing to service the customer.

Afterwards, I went back inside the house to continue the task at hand. My grandmother did not approve of idle time. In my neighborhood, there were lots of children like me who lived with their grandmothers. A major difference between them and me is that they had freedoms that were not afforded to me. I could not leave the yard to walk up the street with a friend because I was always available in case someone needed something from the store. It was definitely not the life of a typical teenager. My life was engulfed by stress, fear, misery, shame, and intimidation.

My grandmother was very strict and regimented. The store had to be open and breakfast had to be ready at 8 AM. On those rare occasions when I overslept, I was greeted with lashes from a switch wielded by my grandmother. It didn't take long for me to learn not to oversleep.

Many afternoons after school, I would walk uptown to pay bills or to purchase store items from the Candy Kitchen. The Candy Kitchen was an establishment that sold wholesale items to be resold retail. I trudged back home with the boxes of candy or cookies I could carry. Uptown was at least a mile from where we lived. It was quite a feat during the summer months when the temperatures are extremely hot in the South.

There was, however, a positive aspect to the trips uptown. The long walks provided me with the exercise I needed to keep me from becoming obese. I was fortunate to have access to lots of candy and cookies that I consumed daily. The trips were also times of freedom and reflection. I was glad to be away from a home where there was no happiness.

For several summers, my grandmother and I cooked meals for transient road workers. Twice a day, we cooked for them—rising early in the morning to make breakfast and serving it before they went off to work. There were probably three or four of them; I have forgotten the exact number.

After breakfast and clean up, my grandmother and I would begin cooking the major meal of the day. The men returned during the afternoon, and we served them dinner.

As a teenager, I felt a great sense of embarrassment. No other family I knew cooked and served food as if their home were a restaurant. The store was always open. In addition to the meal preparation and serving food to those men, I still had to manage the store's operations as people were constantly coming to buy something.

There were also times when white people dropped off their clothes for us to wash. My grandmother and I would hand-wash clothes in tin tubs under a huge pecan tree in the backyard. We would hang the clothes out to dry and later iron them. The white people would return to pick up their clothes and pay a very minimal fee for our labor. My grandmother never gave me any extra money. The only money I was given was for lunch at school and for church on Sundays.

As a young child, I remember thinking that if life became too difficult, I could simply die. No one was aware that I tried to commit suicide while growing up under the care of my grandmother. One day, I decided I wanted to end my miserable life. I mixed insecticide into some coffee. I tried to drink it. Fortunately, it was too gross to drink. I was spared to live on as a warrior who fights for survival every day.

In my moments of despair, I often called out for my mother to come and rescue me. She was never there when I needed a mother. I know she had her own issues; life was not kind to her. I learned at a very early age that the only person I could rely on was myself.

I always had dreams and aspirations for the future. I knew education was the only route out of the miserable life I lived. It was of the utmost importance that I pursue a college degree. I studied and did well in high school. It came as an enormous shock when I was named salutatorian of my high school graduating class. I lacked confidence in myself and my abilities. I convinced myself that the people in charge must have made a mistake. There was no family to gather around me, no voices telling me how proud they were of my achievement. Instead of joy or happiness, I felt only emptiness.

Emancipation Day came when I left home to attend college. But college life was not easy. I struggled with insecurity, and I had low self-esteem. I was afraid to speak up in class, even when I knew the correct answers. I was too afraid to go to the cafeteria alone.

I often felt as though others were looking at me and judging me. I felt shame. I carried shame and a sense of being underprivileged, socially beneath many of my college friends. Many had parents who loved and supported them. I was alone; I had no one. College life was a struggle, but I was strong and I was motivated. I managed to pass every subject, and after four years, I graduated with my BA degree. Despite all odds, I achieved my goal. I received the first of my two college degrees. I was finally proud of an achievement.

After enrolling in college, I never again returned to live with my grandmother permanently. During one of my last visits home from college, however, a significant breaking point occurred between my grandmother and me. I was 19 when I brought home this large fraternity paddle a guy at college had given me. I had always been forced by my grandmother to attend church every Sunday.

The breaking point came on a Sunday morning when I did not want to attend church. I told my grandmother I was not going to church. She picked up that paddle in an attempt to strike me across my back. I grabbed hold of the paddle and informed my grandmother that she could not hit me with it. She backed away with an alarming glare that I translated to mean, "I am done with you!"

I transferred from the college I attended in North Carolina and enrolled in a college in Connecticut. Connecticut is the state where my mother, my aunt, my three uncles, and my brother lived in prior years.

For many years, I carried much guilt because I left my grandmother alone in South Carolina.

I worried constantly about how she would survive without me there to help her. Even though I knew she abused me, I still felt a powerful bond of devotion to her. Walking away pained my heart, for I had long been her loyal and obedient little servant.

My grandmother did survive. One of my uncles sent his three children to live with her for a while. The two younger children stayed about a year before they returned home to their parents.

Apparently, they were unable to adjust to our grandmother's strict rules. The oldest of the three children stayed longer. I am sure she was subjected to much of the same treatment I received. Eventually, she too returned home to Connecticut to be with her parents. After I got married, I returned home yearly to visit my grandmother before she developed dementia. I always left with a heavy heart when it was time to return home to Connecticut. The bond to my grandmother was not broken. My grandmother developed dementia and needed someone to care for her. During her final days, my mother returned from Connecticut to look after her. The bond that had long existed with my maternal grandmother finally ended. It ended the day she died.

I do not know if my grandmother was a narcissist. But I do know that her interactions with me were far from normal. I experienced her physical and emotional abuse. The impact of that abuse has lasting effects on my life. I always knew something was not right with the relationship between my grandmother and me. Perhaps others also noticed something awry in the relationship. I recall a time when one of my uncles boldly asked my grandmother if she hated me. I don't recall her response. Despite the unhappy life I had growing up with my grandmother.

I credit her with shaping my determination, motivation, independence, and endurance. My maternal grandmother was a warrior in her own way. Her strong and forceful impact on my life inspires me to stand tall as the warrior I am today.

A Message To Family And Friends

My heart dictates to me to address family members, friends, neighbors, and acquaintances who know the man I married as being kind, generous, loving, and charming. I want you to know that I honor your experience. I do not question the way the man I married has shown up in your life. I know you see my son as bright, accomplished, loyal, and loving. I do not wish to erase your version of him.

What you saw is not what I lived.

Behind closed doors, I endured something very different, a reality filled with silence, manipulation, emotional cruelty, and deep psychological pain. Not just from the man I married, but eventually from the son I raised. That is the most painful truth I have ever had to face and the most difficult one to share.

I carried this truth in silence for decades. When I tried to speak, I was often met with disbelief, dismissal, or shame. That kind of isolation cuts deeper than words can express. This is my truth. It is the life I lived. It is the pain I survived.

I understand how difficult it may be to believe. The truth is, I would not have believed it either. For 51 years, I lived beside this man and still could not see the full picture. I protected him. I explained away the pain. I believed in the illusion because it was safer than facing the truth. But eventually, the truth became impossible to ignore. I saw it not just in his actions, but in what I became while living under his shadow. I know it may be hard to reconcile the husband and the son you know with the people I describe.

Ask yourself this:

Why would I lie about something so heartbreaking?

What could I possibly gain by exposing the most personal wounds of my life, except for the hope of finally being heard?

The Man I Married

My second slave master was the man I married. I met the man who would become my husband in December 1969. After that fateful meeting, my life was forever changed. This man was the only true love of my life. He exemplified everything I ever dreamed of having in a partner. He was nearly perfection in my eyes. He was the first and only man I experienced the intense intimacy of a sexual relationship. I wholeheartedly admit, the man I married was "the love of my life" until his mask slipped away. The person who had hidden behind the mask for decades emerged, a stranger who did not exemplify the attributes of "the love of my life."

After several months of regular sexual relationships with this man, I became pregnant. I naïvely thought he and I were a couple. I did not know he was seeing other women at the same time. I thought our relationship was special; it most definitely was not. I was merely one of several other women who probably had those same thoughts about their relationship with him. He blatantly told me I should get an abortion. Then he abruptly and completely discarded me as if I never existed. He told me he met someone and they were getting married. I wanted to die; I contemplated suicide. I loved this man so much. I craved for him like a junkie craves drugs. The painful memory of that devastating discard remains with me over five decades later. It was devastation and destruction to the soul of an innocent, vulnerable, and naïve young woman. There is no recovery from what that did to my soul.

I am convinced a higher power sent angels to protect me and to guide me through that crucial time in my life. I made the decision to leave Connecticut during my pregnancy. I contacted my paternal grandmother, whom I did not know very well, having met her only once. She welcomed me to her home. My paternal grandmother was the polar opposite of my maternal grandmother. She welcomed me and showered me with genuine kindness throughout my pregnancy, never judging me in any way.

My son's father did not marry the other woman. I do not know what happened to that relationship. Many years later, I questioned him about her. His response, "She was a real bitch." I recall feeling relief hearing his response; she apparently was not better than me. Those were my thoughts before I acquired education about the ploys of narcissists. Knowledge brought awareness that it is common for a narcissist to vocalize negative comments about former relationships. The fault is never with the narcissist; the fault is always found with the other person in the relationship.

When I got back to Connecticut, I contacted my son's father. He invited our new baby boy and me to visit him at his apartment. His greeting toward us was a performance of kindness and care. I did not feel a sense of love emanating from him to our son and me. That was a huge red flag that I chose to dismiss. My unfortunate state of mind was that I still loved this man who had so brutally and cruelly abandoned me during the months when I desperately needed him. The love sickness I had for him consumed me and made me feel elated to be back in his presence. My instincts registered a red flag, but my heart ignored the warning. I was living in my mother's home. One night, my son's father convinced me to stay overnight at his apartment. My mother adamantly disapproved of me staying overnight at his apartment. I did not need any more drama in my life. I needed to get back to my teaching position so that I could provide for my son and myself. Something inside of me changed after giving birth to my son. I told my son's father there would be no more visits to his apartment. I was done.

I loved my baby's father dearly, but I loved my son more. His father had already shown me a side of himself that was beyond my understanding. How could a man so easily abandon the woman who is carrying his son and move on without a care in the world? What is normal about that? His behavior was not so different from what my father had done years earlier. That is not the behavior of the norm; that is the behavior of a narcissist. They only care about what benefits them. Narcissists treat people like disposable objects that they can easily replace. The narcissist's devaluation of another human being can be merciless and cruel. The narcissist has no compassion and no empathy for victims.

My studies of narcissism taught me that this is typical behavior exhibited by a narcissist. It is part of the vicious cycle of idealization, devaluation, and discard. It is not personal; it is merely how a narcissist operates in every relationship. Victims of narcissistic abuse must understand this dynamic of narcissistic abuse. I had a new focus in life; I was a mother. I wanted to be the best mother I could be for my son, providing him with the love and protection I had never received. I wanted him to feel secure in the world. Then, suddenly out of the blue, the man who was to become my husband came to see me. I was really surprised. I honestly did not expect to ever hear from him again.

The months of discard and abandonment were still fresh wounds. I was ready to move forward in another direction. He took me for a ride to talk. During that fateful ride, he stated, "We need to get blood tests so we can get married." That was the proposal from the man I foolishly married. I was so gullible, so naïve, and so innocent; I joyously agreed. I was foolishly thinking, "He must truly love me." It was inconceivable to me that anyone could actually marry a person whom they do not love. I now know a narcissist does not love; they dominate and they control. I was not loved; I was easily dominated and easily controlled like a slave. Throughout the following years, I would laugh as I shared my story of the strange and unusual proposal. Today, I feel shame and embarrassment. The story reflects how little I valued myself. I was always willing to settle for the bare minimum this man offered me in every situation. The bare minimum is exactly what I received for the next five decades.

I married this man just a few weeks after returning to Connecticut. There had been no contact with him during my pregnancy. I am sure other women were heartbroken when he married me. They were probably as much in love with him as I was, but he chose me. I am not sure why I was the chosen one. I know it had nothing to do with love for me. I must have offered some benefit that the others did not. I feel so disgusted that I allowed myself to be lured into a relationship with such a deceptive predator. I was his chosen prey for that moment in time. When I signed that marriage license, I instantly became the property and ownership of the man I married. I was officially his slave. I was totally under his control for the next five decades of my life.

I was masterfully deceived. The marriage was the lure of a devious and deceptive covert narcissist. He never connected with me as a loving wife. I was merely the stupid slave he could easily control. I recall a time when he boldly told me that I was stupid for not knowing who he is. That is what he truly thought of me. This is a painful realization of truth. I'm a member of several online support groups. Victims share heartbreaking stories about narcissistic, abusive experiences. A narcissist, with no remorse or regret, can walk away leaving behind wife and children. I heard stories from victims who were destroyed mentally, emotionally, and financially. Their stories make me feel as if I am fortunate in some aspects. I relate to the emotional and mental abuse too well; but to some degree, I was spared the financial destruction that others experienced. The man I married always put our assets in both our names. Our cars and homes were always in both our names. I never discovered any separate accounts. The ones I was aware of were all joint. I feel blessed that he did not destroy me financially. He could have easily taken everything from the version of me I was decades ago. I was so blinded by my love for him that I would have signed anything he placed in front of me.

I never question the man I married about money. I completely trusted whatever he said or did. I thought he was smart. I thought he was always making the best decisions for us. Now, I know I was living in a fantasy world where deception lingered in every aspect of my life. The man I married was the master of deception. I slowly became aware that he spent large sums of money on himself. I suspect he also spent a lot of money entertaining other women. He admitted to picking up women at strip clubs and having sex with them in our car. How much of our money was spent on those women, I will never know. I do know that lots of money disappeared, but I never questioned what became of it. The man I married was in charge, I had been programmed not to ask. I trusted the person who did not have my best interests at his heart.

A covert narcissist masterfully deceived me. There was never any "us" in our relationship. The relationship was just about "him." Everything in our decades together was done in an arena where he was the star, all revolved around him. I was his slave stagehand who catered to his wants and needs.

The man I married used me; he verbally and psychologically abused me. He meticulously tormented me with his subtle acts of manipulation, gaslighting, projection, and deception. He successfully molded me to be who he wanted me to be. I wandered around lost in a fog of confusion. I never mattered. I existed in the delusional world of a covert narcissist for five decades. The illusion that we were a married couple has been shattered. He was never my husband. He is: The Man I Married.

The man I married enjoyed a happy, carefree life away from home. He stayed out late on weekends. Sometimes he did not come home at all. Sometimes he went missing on holidays. I existed in a constant state of confusion and anxiety. I was struggling to survive in a world of horror created by a cheating and deceptive, disordered man. This man enjoyed his happy, carefree life for five decades at the expense of my physical, emotional, mental, and financial well-being. That is the callous behavior of a narcissist. That is the role a devious and deceptive narcissist plays in the lives of innocent people with no remorse and no regret.

People are enthralled by his good looks and his charm. They believed his lies. I admit that his good looks and charm enthralled me, and I believed his lies for decades. His character is impressive, impeccable, and overwhelmingly charming in public. People will never believe the truth about this man's character behind closed doors; he is a master of disguise. It is frustrating, heartbreaking, and sickening to witness his masked performance in public. I know the truth. It is revealed behind closed doors.

I lived the horror of his manipulation and deception, not understanding what was happening to me. It became my normal. I understand so much more about what happened in this relationship. I can see so clearly now that the fog has lifted. The man I married projected all his negativity onto me. What was lacking in him, he methodically made me feel that it was lacking in me. It was as if we exchanged identities. He became me, and I became him. It was done by design. It was subtle and insidious. He would say, "We are one." I ignorantly thought that meant our relationship was so uniquely special. The narcissist was stating that he had power and control over me. I was his humble, loyal, and obedient slave. I bowed down to all his commands.

I am in awe of the fact that I lived with this man for nearly 54 years. I have no idea who this strange person is. I look at him, and the question comes to mind, "Who are you?" The image I see physically is the man I loved for decades. However, I have no idea who he is; he is a complex and fearful stranger. I fear what he is capable of doing to me. My instincts tell me there is something undoubtedly devious and unsettling about him. How could I not know all these years? This man always hated me; he hid his hatred behind the mask of fake love. I reflect on past events; I clearly see it. It was there all those years, but I was too blind to see. He made me feel as if I were the fortunate one to be with him. He made me feel dumb, unworthy, and ugly. He made me feel like I was privileged to be his wife. I cannot explain how he did it, but I know it was done by his words and by his actions. He was insidiously clever. He made me feel fearful; he made me feel insecure. I only felt safe when he was in charge; he was always right. He knew how to fix everything in every situation. I was always obedient; I willfully followed him like a sheep led to slaughter. He had me entrenched in a bubble surrounded by a never-ending fog of confusion. He kept me there for decades, trapped in a state of chaos. I am shocked and saddened by memories of that version of me. I weep for her and I weep for her struggles of survival all those years. She was a warrior who was protected by forces in the Universe.

When the man I married knew he had me securely locked in that bubble, he discarded me. He viewed me as worthless. His words and actions toward me were bitter and cruel. My body, my mind, and my soul endured unrelenting pain. The ongoing abuse caused havoc on my body. My hair fell out. I developed skin problems. I developed thyroid problems. Pain developed in my legs that made it excruciatingly painful to move around and to walk any distance. I cried constantly; I had suicidal thoughts. I remembered my childhood thought: "You can always just die if life becomes too difficult." I wanted the man I married to erase my pain; to make things better like he always had in the past. No, that was not happening, not this time. He displayed no compassion for my pain. My time with him had expired!

There is always an expiration date when you are in a narcissistic relationship. Victims are easily replaceable commodities for a narcissist. The man I married decided my time had expired and he intensified the abuse. He rejected me physically and emotionally; he called me awful names; he criticized me. He said I was too negative. I believed him. I tried to be a better person. I doubled down and tried desperately to please him. I cooked special meals for him. I displayed much affection toward him. There was no reciprocity. Nothing fazed him. He ignored me. He stonewalled me. He grew silent. My time with the narcissist had expired.

I wanted to die. In my heart, I believe he wanted me to commit suicide. However, I believe a higher power kept those angels ever-present to protect me. I thought constantly of my precious grandchildren. I needed to stay alive for them. Through it all, I stood tall as a warrior, like my maternal grandmother's influence taught me to be.

Over time, the man I married, in a devious and crafty manner, has successfully devastated and destroyed the relationship between our son and me. My son is cold-hearted toward me. My son uses the same tactics from the narcissistic playbook that his father uses. My son tries to gaslight me and confuse me. He disrespects me by calling me by my given name in his effort to diminish me. He does not care about my well-being. He told me I am not welcome at his house. I have no contact with my son because I need to protect my mental and physical health; he is harmful to me. My son's uncanny behavior is devastatingly painful. It cannot be normal for a son to cause harm to the mother who nurtured, loved, and cared for him. My son displays very strong narcissistic traits. He is a mirror of his father.

I love my son, and I love the man I married. I was a loyal and faithful wife. I strived to be a good mother. I worked full-time as a teacher for over three decades. I never saw the monthly paycheck I earned. I gave the man I married full access to my paycheck every month without question. I never doubted nor questioned his use of it. I asked for very little and I spent very little. I was frugal; the man I married was not frugal. I was obedient, submissive, loyal, and honest for over five decades. The man I married was not loyal nor honest. I was his obediently ignorant slave; he was my abusive master.

Life happens. I lived for decades in this abusive marriage. I thought it was a normal marriage because I did not know what a normal marriage was supposed to look like or how it functioned. As time progresses, the abuse becomes more blatant. The man I married is cold and distant. There is no affection, no intimacy, no connection, and no communication between us. He does not talk to me. He rejects me and ignores me as if I do not exist. We go to a restaurant, we sit there, and we eat without uttering a word. That is gut-wrenchingly painful. I look around and see couples who appear happily engaged with each other.

It triggers depression; it triggers grief. I feel physical pain. I breathe, but I do not feel alive.

The silent treatment has become a way of life in our household. The man I married only engages in conversation with me if it is of necessity. This creates feelings of devastation and destruction that cannot be described. This is not the way humans were created to live. This is not the way I want to live. It is a life of devastation and destruction.

There are endless days when I look in the mirror and wonder why I was never good enough for the man I married. The thought torments my soul. I never felt beautiful enough. I never felt smart enough. I never felt worthy enough. I see other women and think wow, she looks like someone he would have treated better. It sickens me that I think that way. It is hard not to, after years of being devalued. The origin of those thoughts grew from seeds of doubt planted by the man I married season after season. I may not be the woman he wanted, but I am the woman who survived him. I am the lone standing warrior. That makes me more than enough.

There are so many people with stories to tell about narcissistic abuse. I hear some stories that are far worse than mine. We all experience the narcissistic cycles of idealization, devaluation, and discard. In long-term relationships like mine, the cycles are repeated over and over until the victim finally becomes aware of what is happening and makes a change.

Narcissistic abuse comes in cycles. I was trapped in a pattern of these repeated cycles for decades. The patterns kept me confused and emotionally dependent. The cycles begin with idealization. This is when the narcissist is most charming, loving, affectionate, and generous. This cycle does not last. The next cycle is devaluation. This is when the cruelty begins. You are criticized, ignored, controlled, manipulated, and deceived. You become lost in a maze of confusion, wondering what is happening. The final cycle is the discard cycle.

This is a brutally cruel cycle. It is when you get dehumanized. You receive the silent treatment. You are often ignored and rejected. There is limited intimacy or none at all. The narcissist emotionally detaches. Some narcissists will physically abandon you and move on with someone as if you never existed. Your mind struggles to process what happened. There is never closure.

The man I married never physically abandoned the home. He remained in the home and tormented me with these repeated cycles as I struggled for decades to understand the complexity of our relationship. I have learned there are many people existing in the world who have personality disorders. I know I do not have the credentials to diagnose anyone; there is no denial of that fact. I am sure I will be criticized and judged for making such a radical assessment.

However, I believe without any doubt, the man I married has NPD, narcissistic personality disorder. Everything I have heard, I have seen, I have felt, and I have experienced with the man I married paints a vivid picture of NPD. Only those of us who have experienced narcissistic abuse know the truth. This is my truth. These people have no empathy and no love for other human beings. They are experts at deception. Their primary focus is on themselves. They destroy the people who love them the most. The behaviors of this man have devastated my soul. My only crime is that I loved him too much. My sentence has been five decades of narcissistic abuse.

In this life with the man I married, "I breathe, but I do not feel alive."

Torment on Hilton Head Island

I was married to him for fifty-one years before I fully realized that the man I married was abusing me. We were living on Hilton Head Island at the time. For many years, the marriage had been emotionally empty, but I was in denial because I loved this man so deeply. I wanted to believe he loved me back, but during those years on Hilton Head Island, something inside him turned even colder. The verbal abuse became sudden, jarring, and cruel. He called me a "nasty bitch" and told me I was possessed. I remember staring at him in shock, thinking, "Where is this coming from?" "What did I do wrong?" I now understand it was not sudden at all. It was the moment his mask began to slip, and I was shown who had been lurking behind it all along.

We were members of a Qi Gong group at the time. I had learned about it from a friend and attended a session alone. Then, wanting to share something good, I brought the man I married along. He was charming and magnetic. He quickly rose to a place of admiration and influence within the group. I was so proud of him. Over time, I felt a strange shift. He began to distance himself from me during the group gatherings. While he was warm and jovial with others, he became ice-cold with me. On the ride home, he would retreat into silence, treating me as if I were invisible.

After each Qi Gong session, I felt more erased. My presence felt like an inconvenience. Eventually, I stopped going to the sessions, not because anyone told me to leave, but because I could no longer bear the emotional rejection. I felt pushed out by the man I married. The very person I introduced to the group was now the admired star performer on a stage I helped build. He flourished in my absence. The group met three days a week. He had regular lunches and social outings with them. They adored him. I was left home alone, discarded, erased, grieving, and unraveling.

I was also under the care of a psychiatrist then, but all she did was give me medication. No one truly saw what I was enduring. I was crumbling inside. I began taking long walks by myself sometimes for miles, hoping the rhythm of my steps would bring me peace. I would cry as I walked, silently begging for the pain to stop. Then one day, a strange and debilitating pain seized my legs. It came out of nowhere. The walking stopped. The one outlet I had to soothe my mind was gone. I began physical therapy, but the pain persisted. I often wondered if it was my body screaming out what my voice could not.

Desperate to escape the emotional pain, I would drive to a Walmart parking lot, crawl into the backseat of my car, and cry until there were no more tears left. That back seat became my sanctuary. I sat there, broken, invisible, praying for some kind of relief, hoping that someone, something, would save me.

Meanwhile, the man I married moved along each day with ease. He had his Qi Gong group. He had his fans. I strongly suspect, though I cannot prove, that he had someone else who had captured his attention, a younger woman in the Qigong group. He talked about her a lot and was always helping her. He was vibrant and alive. I was fading.

I made the decision to move back to Georgia. I believe a higher power led me to pack up and to leave. I believe I would have died on that island if I had stayed. He was slowly erasing my existence without ever lifting a hand. His cruelty did the work. His weapon was invisibility. His violence was silence. His aim was my disappearance.

I will never recover from what happened to me during those years on Hilton Head Island. Even now, the memories haunt me. The smiles he wore in public while destroying me in private. The group that embraced him while I dissolved into nothingness. The loneliness, the isolation, the torment; it was all there on Hilton Head Island, South Carolina. It was where the man I married ceased to exist. The stranger who had always been lurking behind the mask finally revealed himself in full. I feel blessed to have survived to tell my story.

If Only It Were Truth

While living on Hilton Head Island in 2021, I was in a place of deep pain. The man I married had grown distant, cold, and unreachable. I felt invisible and ached to be acknowledged, to be seen, to be loved. I begged him to write me something, anything. This is what he wrote:

My Dear Veronica, Always and Forever

Veronica,

I have always been close to you in one form or another. The first time I laid eyes on you, I had an unusual feeling that we would somehow be united.

While we were together or separated during our relationship, there was always something that bound us together. I have always loved you and felt the need to care for and be with you. I love you more than you can imagine, you are my core and soul.

Always,

(His name)

At the time, my heart believed it. It gave me a moment of peace, a flicker of hope. For a little while, it eased the loneliness. But now, I read it with different eyes; eyes opened by truth. I see the contradiction between words and actions. Still, a part of me mourns what could have been. A part of me still whispers: If only it were truth.

He Made Me Feel Ugly

He never said I was ugly. I felt it in the way he looked past me. I felt it as his eyes wandered to other women with interest. I felt it in the way he barely touched me, barely complimented me, barely saw me at all. There were times I looked at my reflection and whispered, *"Why would anyone love this?"* There were moments so dark, I believed I was too ugly to live.

This is what long-term narcissistic abuse does. It does not just hurt your heart, it destroys your image of yourself. There is a silence so cruel, it convinces you you are nothing. When you live for years beside a man who never truly sees you, never values your presence, you begin to vanish. Your posture collapses. Your eyes lose their spark. Your body ages under the weight of being constantly unloved. I became this way after loving a man who was incapable of loving me back. *He made me feel ugly.*

To any woman reading this who feels the same: You are not alone. You are not broken. You are not ugly. You are a survivor of being unseen. One day, whether you leave or simply wake up inside your own truth, you will begin to see the woman you were before he told you who to be.

The Illusion

There is an indescribable kind of pain that comes from loving someone who never truly existed. I shared a home with a man I called husband, a man who performed kindness and goodwill in public; a man who appeared composed and confident to everyone he encountered. However, behind closed doors, he was often absent, dismissive, and cold.

For years, I questioned myself instead of him. That is what living beside a narcissist does. He conditioned me to doubt my instincts and to feel guilty for noticing the truth. He did not need to attack me or to challenge me. He just needed to keep me confused. And confused I remained for decades.

There were many betrayals. He never left a trail of evidence; there were only gut feelings. A deep, gnawing sense that something was wrong. I could not attach a name to it. That unnamed feeling tormented me for decades. I always sensed something I could not prove. There were no visible betrayals. There was silence. There was denial. There was emotional starvation. Now I know I was consistently being deceived and betrayed while being told everything was fine. Every time I came close to seeing the truth, he retreated behind his mask, staying calm, rational, and untouchable. I stood lost in the shadows of my own doubts.

Narcissistic abuse slowly unravels your sense of self in the presence of someone who does not see you and does not hear you. That is the truth that confuses and pains the hearts and minds of victims enduring narcissistic abuse.

I often asked myself: How did I not know sooner? How could I live five decades beside someone I never truly knew? Today, I have a better understanding.

The abuse was not just in what he did. It was in what he withheld: truth, connection, acknowledgment of my reality. He was never my husband. He was an illusion. I was living a life filled with grief, pain, and confusion in what was all disguised as a marriage. The husband and wife portrait looked real. It never was; it was an illusion.

He Gave Me An STD

He brought home a sexually transmitted disease to me. That was over 25 years ago, and I did not leave. I should have. That kind of betrayal should have shattered the foundation of our marriage, but it did not. We lived like nothing happened, as if I had not just been violated by the man I trusted most. I was too broken to react. I was too conditioned to silence and fear of abandonment.

So I swallowed the truth and carried the shame. The shame that was not mine to carry. The shame that was his. Yet, I wore it like a second skin heavy, silent, and suffocating. I took his sickness into my body and his guilt into my soul. He just moved on untouched and unfazed by the enormity of the devastation and destruction he left in my body and to my mind. I still do not understand why I did not leave.

Looking back, it is like watching another woman, a version of me that I barely recognize. The woman I am today would never take him back, not after such a monumental betrayal. I did not know then what I know now. If I had, my life would have taken a different path.

The Cycle of Replacement

There is a pattern in the man I married's family, a legacy of abandonment and moving on. The repetition is undeniable. The man I married's mother divorced his father. His father married his mistress as soon as the divorce papers were signed. Just like that, a new woman stepped into the role of wife. There was no time for grief, no reflection, and no accountability. There was simply replacement.

Years later, the pattern repeated with our son. His marriage ended. He immediately married the woman he had been in a relationship with. A new woman inserted into the story before the first had even stepped fully out of frame.

Now I look at my own life, and I realize I am caught in the very same cycle. The man I married has said many times that our relationship is over. He does not hide it. He seems to feel no remorse. He blames me for everything and positions himself as the one who endured. I believe in my heart that he wanted me gone when we lived on Hilton Head Island. He had my replacement, a younger woman. He did not have the financial means to sustain that relationship with me in the picture.

If I were removed from the earth, his financial state would have improved. That is the reason his cruelty was unrelenting. He wanted me gone. My life did not matter. What he wanted and desired was all that mattered. That knowledge devastates and destroys me.

This is generational. This is how the men in this family operate, leaving behind one woman and placing another into her role as if loyalty were irrelevant and women are interchangeable. I am not interchangeable. I am no longer blind. I see the pattern. I lived the pattern. I will not protect it with my silence.

This story of betrayal does not end with another woman merely being erased and replaced.

This time, it ends with a woman speaking her truth.

Why He Never Left Me

Narcissists are known for discarding their spouses. They get bored and want someone new and exciting. They will often leave for the other person. The person who makes them feel powerful, desired, and admired. Sometimes the new person is kept in secrecy. Other times, they will boldly leave you for this person who has captivated them; there is no warning or preparation. You are left in a state of confusion. In many cases, the discard happens quickly and brutally.

The man I married did not leave. He stayed for five decades. I took that to mean something. I thought maybe we were different. Now I understand. He did not stay because he loved me. He stayed because I was useful. He did not need to leave. He had comfort, stability, and a loyal wife who asked for nothing.

I continued to work for three years after he retired. During that time, I willingly gave him over $240,000 of my saved teacher retirement from two previous states. When I retired from the third state, I added my modest pension to our household without hesitation. I never questioned anything because I believed we were building a life together. That is what kept him in the marriage. It was never love nor commitment; it was convenience.

To any woman reading this:

Do not assume that because he stays, he cares.

Do not assume that decades mean devotion.

Do not assume that silence means safety.

Ask questions.

Know your rights.

Protect your money.

And above all, pay attention to what his actions reveal, not just what he says.

Sometimes the most dangerous narcissist is the one who stays.

He quietly drains your life, your trust, and your future. That is my experience. That is my truth.

Caged by Obligation

There is a kind of pain that does not scream. It sits inside you, slowly devastating and destroying your life. There is an expressive message of knowing you must leave, but feeling chained by love, loyalty, history, and the word "family."

I live with a man who frightens me. His voice can cut through me like a blade. His silence is colder than winter. His eyes look at me like I am nothing. And yet, I stay. I stay because I vowed to be his wife. I stay because we have lived a lifetime together. I stay because we are family. I stay because I feel an obligation to the marriage.

I have begun to realize that obligation is not love, not safety, or peace for me. It has become a cage, a prison made of guilt, vows, shared name, finances, and expectations. It is a cage where I am slowly fading away; the essence of me is slowly being erased. "I breathe, but I do not feel alive."

Now that the mask has been removed, the man I married no longer has to perform in my presence. He shows me who he truly is. He is cruel and unpredictable. Sometimes I believe he is dangerous. Yet, I still view him as my family, and that is what makes it so hard to just walk away.

To any woman reading this who is torn between duty and survival: You are not alone.

You are not weak for staying, and you are not cruel if you choose to go.

You are allowed to grieve the man you once believed in and still choose yourself in the end.

Sometimes, the bravest thing we can do is: leave the cage.

A Letter To The Man I Married

Dear Man I Married,

I once believed you were my partner, my protector, my future. I gave you my youth, my devotion, my trust, and my love for over fifty years. I loved you through the silence, the cruelty, the indifference, the betrayals. You took all I had to give.

I transformed myself to be enough for you, to keep the peace, to avoid the punishments, to survive your shifting moods, and cold disdain.

I remember so many nights I lay awake, waiting for the sound of your car in the early hours of the morning. You would return home without explanation, slide into bed, turn your back to me, and fall asleep. I cried and felt deeply wounded; I felt as if I did not exist.

I remember the times we argued in the car. I told you to let me out. You did, without hesitation. You left me alone on city streets with no phone and no way home. You drove away and never looked back. I remember the painful times on Hilton Head Island when I got on my knees to embrace you, to beg for comfort, for closeness, and you smiled coldly, patting me on the back like a pet dog. I remember when we moved back to Georgia.

I wanted to support you, to help you make friends and find purpose. I walked through neighborhoods, going door to door to start a Qi Gong group for you. When I reminded you of that effort, your only response was: "I did not ask you to do it." These were not isolated incidents. This was a pattern, a deliberate stripping away of my dignity, year after year.

The deepest wound you inflicted was not just against me; it was against our son. You poisoned his mind against me. You turned him away from the one person who loved him without condition. You took my child and severed the sacred bond between mother and son. I watched, helpless, as you distorted his reality and used him as a weapon not only to hurt me, but to control him, too. In doing so, you did not just devastate my life, you damaged our son's.

I am not the same woman you married. She is gone, buried beneath the years of pretending, pleasing, and performing. In her place stands someone you never expected: a woman with a voice, a spine, and a pen. I regret the time I lost, not because I loved you, but because I did not love myself enough to walk away sooner.

I write this letter not to forgive, not to reconcile, not to soften the truth, but to reclaim what was stolen from me: my story, my clarity, my worth. You did not break me. You tried, but I am still here. I speak not just for myself, I speak for every woman who has begged for crumbs of love from a man who had no love to give. I speak for every woman who stayed too long, hoping the coldness would thaw, that one day he would see her, value her, love her. I speak for every woman who has been silenced, discarded, and blamed.

I let go of the illusion. I release the pain. I carry forward with the strength I found in speaking my truth. I write this not as your wife, but as the woman who survived you.

Veronica Harvin

If you are a woman struggling in a narcissistic relationship, reading this, hear me now: You do not have to spend your life trying to be loved by someone who cannot love. You are not the problem. You are not crazy. You are not invisible. You are worthy. You are enough. You are not alone.

Why Did He Abuse Me?

After writing everything in this section, I still find myself asking the question:

Why did he do this to me for so long? How could someone sleep beside me, eat beside me, and walk through life with me for 54 years be so emotionally detached and so cruel?

The answer, I now understand, lies in something called Narcissistic Personality Disorder (NPD). It is not just selfishness. It is not just arrogance. It is a disorder of the personality; a deep psychological wound that affects how a person sees themselves, others, and the world.

The man I married did not love me the way most people understand love. He was not capable of emotional empathy. He did not form deep, secure attachments. His entire identity was shaped by the need to be in control, admired, and never questioned. I loved him and I trusted him; I became the perfect mirror. When I stopped reflecting on what he wanted to see, I became the enemy.

That is how narcissistic abuse works.

Narcissistic Personality Disorder

Narcissistic Personality Disorder is a condition characterized by:

- A grandiose sense of self-importance

- A deep need for admiration and validation

- A lack of empathy for the feelings of others

- An inability to take responsibility for harm caused

- Extreme sensitivity to criticism or rejection

- A pattern of manipulation, blame-shifting, and control

People with NPD often create a public persona of being confident, generous, charming, and charismatic. While behind closed doors, they are being cold, critical, or detached from the ones who love them. They cannot tolerate vulnerability, so they reject any real emotional closeness. They cannot face shame, so they rewrite the truth to protect themselves. They cannot give real love because they are too focused on themselves and preserving their false image.

The Narcissist

A narcissist is a person who has an excessive interest or admiration for himself/herself. They believe the world revolves around them. There is a common consensus that a narcissist is that loud, arrogant, self-centered, life of the party type of person. Yes, that describes the overt narcissist. There is another type, one much harder to see. The covert narcissist hides in plain sight.

This person appears kind, helpful, loving, loyal, honest, and even humble. They offer a helping hand. They show up. They perform so well that even those living in the same house do not know who is lurking behind the mask. This is the covert narcissist, the one who does not appear flashy or boastful. This one is quiet, subtle, calculating, deceitful, and cruel. The people closest to the covert narcissist endure a hidden form of abuse: the silence, the sarcasm, the criticism, the gaslighting, the icy withdrawal, the emotional punishments.

The covert narcissist is a master of resentment. They often resent the people who they claim to love; the spouse who needs support; the children who require attention; the family who expects empathy. Many victims of narcissistic abuse live with a covert narcissist without knowing the truth for years and even decades, like me. Why? We know there is something wrong, but we have no name for it. We deceived ourselves to justify the behaviors and actions of the person we love.

We make excuses. When the mask slips away, we seek answers. We research for knowledge.

One day, the terrifying truth is revealed: This person is a narcissist! We realize we have been on a journey to devastation and destruction.

Trait	**Description**
Exploitive	Belittles others
Envious	Displays arrogance
Deceptive	Focuses on fantasy
Manipulative	Has no boundaries
Sense of entitlement	Needs admiration
Lacks empathy	

I witness and experience the calamitous side effects victims undergo when you are in a relationship with a narcissistic person. The damaging side effects are spawned from the narcissist's embodiment and exposition of these self-centered traits.

Does a narcissist know he/she is a narcissist? I have not done enough research to know the answer. I believe the man I married knows there is something odd about himself. He once stated to me in reference to himself, "I am not human." That statement sent chills through my body. I recall my son referring to himself as an alien. I offer no discernment on those statements. I just think they are of interest. I mistakenly called out the man I married as a narcissist. That prompted our son to research narcissism. Our son concluded that I am the narcissist.

Lee Hammock is a proclaimed, diagnosed self-aware narcissist. According to Lee Hammock, a narcissist knows he/she is different. He says he always knew something was different about himself. He states he did not connect with people in the ways he witnessed other people connecting. He says he mimicked and mirrored the good behaviors of people he met in life to become the person he is today.

"Narcissists are like a wonder of the universe—rare, unique, and special. Their minds are complex and layered, but their hearts are missing something vital. They exist on a strange edge of humanity: dangerous not because of their strength, but because of their emptiness."

Narcissistic Supply

For the narcissist, supply is as vital as air or food. It is the fuel that keeps their fragile ego alive. Supply can come in many forms. It can be admiration, fear, obedience, attention, or even outrage. It can be public praise or private submission. It can be the smile of a stranger, the envy of a peer, or the devotion of a partner.

When the narcissist's supply is another person, a lover, an affair partner, or a string of hidden relationships, the wound it creates in their spouse cuts deep. It is not just about physical betrayal. It is a massive level of disrespect and disloyalty. It is about watching the person you loved use your pain to feed their own need for power and validation. It is knowing they can smile at you while holding someone else in their heart or in their bed.

The man I married once told me, without shame, that he had sex in our car with women he picked up at strip clubs. It was not just the act that crushed me. It was the way he used the confession like another weapon, knowing the image would burn in my mind. In that moment, my heartbreak became his nourishment. For the narcissist, this is not romance. It is consumption. They will take from anyone, at any cost, to keep themselves fed.

Narcissistic Alliance

A narcissistic alliance happens when two or more narcissists or a narcissist and an ally join forces to target, control, or discredit a victim. It is not built on love, but on mutual benefit and the exchange of narcissistic supply. It often involves coordinated gaslighting, smear campaigns, and presenting a united front to outsiders. Together, they reinforce each other's lies and isolate the victim from support.

In my life, the man I married and our son formed such an alliance. Their bond was not father-son closeness, it was built on undermining me. They shared and supported false stories, erased my voice, and found common ground in betrayal.

One of their most damaging moves was bringing in an outsider, Martha Pike, who accepted their version of events without ever knowing the truth. Based solely on what she was told, Martha Pike gave a diagnosis that questioned my sanity. A diagnosis, the man I married and our son then used as a weapon against me. Martha Pike's willingness to play a role in their deception made her part of the alliance, whether she realized it or not.

When two people you love join forces against you, the pain is doubled. When they enlist others to join their cause, it becomes a wall of lies almost impossible to break through.

Flying Monkeys

Flying monkeys are the willing or unwitting helpers who carry out the narcissist's agenda. They may be family members, friends, coworkers, or acquaintances recruited to deliver hurtful messages, gather information, spread lies, or apply pressure to the victim. Like the winged creatures sent by the *Wicked Witch in The Wizard of Oz*, they attack from a distance, doing the narcissist's bidding without the narcissist having to get their own hands dirty. While a narcissistic alliance is the larger strategic partnership, the network of relationships the narcissist builds to maintain power, image, and control, flying monkeys are the foot soldiers within that alliance. The alliance is the army; the flying monkeys are the ones sent on missions to enforce the narcissist's will.

In my life, the only flying monkey I am aware of is our son. He has been used to deliver hurtful words, repeated lies, and to intimidate me into silence, all while he, the man I married, remains in the background, appearing calm and innocent. Through our son, the man I married could inflict emotional harm without having to confront me directly.

The Narcissistic Home

Life in a narcissistic home can be traumatizing. It is a place where fear lingers behind kindness, and smiles conceal pain. It is a place ruled by control, manipulation, and secrets. One person dominates and another submits.

The narcissistic home is where children can become collateral damage. They are sometimes assigned rigid and damaging roles: the Golden Child and the Scapegoat. The Golden Child is praised, protected, and held up as a reflection of the narcissist's false image. Their worth is based on loyalty, obedience, and their ability to uphold the family's façade. The Scapegoat, on the other hand, is criticized, blamed, and emotionally abandoned. They learn early that their feelings do not matter and that speaking out will only bring punishment. These roles are not born from truth or merit, but from the narcissist's need to control and divide. While the Golden Child may appear favored, their acceptance is conditional, and they live in quiet fear of losing that status. The Scapegoat, though vilified, often becomes the truth-teller, the one who sees the abuse for what it is. Both roles leave deep and lasting scars, ensuring that even siblings are pitted against each other rather than united against the real source of harm.

When my son was four years old, his older brother died. My son grew up in an only child household. He was raised in a house where two emotional worlds existed and collided. He was a child caught in an emotional crossfire. His father demanded obedience and loyalty. There were no threats, just subtle domination and conditional approval. My son learned that love was transactional and unpredictable. Then there was me. I tried to absorb pain and to keep peace where there was none. I thought I was protecting him, but I was teaching him that love means tolerating pain, staying quiet, and making sacrifices for someone else's comfort.

There were no siblings to compare notes. No one to confirm what was confusing, painful, or wrong. My son endured both center of attention and complete aloneness. I see now how this affected him, how it shaped his choices, his relationships, and even the way he sees me.

Narcissistic Splitting

Splitting is a defense mechanism where a person sees others as either entirely good or entirely bad, with no middle ground. Narcissists use it to protect their fragile self-image. When you meet their needs, you are "all good," When you disappoint or challenge them, you become "all bad." There is no room for a balanced view, and the shift can happen instantly.

I lived through this with the man I married.

One day, I was everything to him, the perfect wife, the woman who stood by him through it all. The next day, I was the problem, the source of his misery, the enemy in his own home. There was no in-between. He could not see me as a human being with both strengths and flaws;

I was either "all good" or "all bad," depending on how well I met his needs or stayed in my place.

Living in this constant swing was exhausting. I found myself trying harder and harder to hold onto the "good" version of me in his eyes, even as the "bad" version was dragged out and punished. Over time, his splitting became my confusion, until I could barely recognize my own worth outside of how he chose to see me that day.

The Quiet Terror

Living with a narcissistic spouse can be a painful and terrifying existence. It is not always obvious nor dramatic. It is quiet and subtle in ways that only those who live it understand. Inside the home, the spouse learns to adjust her tone, her words, and her expressions just to keep him calm. She walks softly and quietly because she is afraid of the shift in his voice, the cold silence, the subtle punishments.

I lived this way for decades. I thought if I stayed calm, cooked the meals, played the role assigned to me, he would be content. No matter how hard I tried, it was never enough. A narcissist does not want peace. They want power. I stayed quiet. I smiled when my heart was aching. I gave love unconditionally. I longed and hoped just maybe he would reciprocate. He rarely did. Nothing was ever enough. A narcissist does not seek love. He seeks control. The presence of the man I married generates fear. It is just like the fear I felt long ago in the presence of my maternal grandmother. When I am away from his presence, I can breathe. I can think clearly. I can function better. It was always that way throughout every year that we have been together. His absence brings more peace than his presence ever does. Narcissistic fear is a quiet terror that settles into your body, creating much anxiety and often panic attacks. I took medication for over thirty years to manage the fear and the anxiety that never left me. I thought I was the issue; I thought that I had mental issues.

Now I know it was my home environment that was impacting my mental state. It was the constant exposure to gaslighting, control, manipulation, deception, and emotional detachment. I never felt safe and secure.

"My home, with the man I married, always was and continues to be, a place of fear."

Narcissistic Envy

Envy is at the heart of so much of the destruction that narcissists cause. It is not the kind of envy that most people feel. It is not that fleeting feeling of jealousy when someone else has something you wish you had. Narcissistic envy is darker. It is corrosive. It fuels cruelty.

The narcissist does not just envy what you have; they envy who you are. They envy your ability to love, your capacity for empathy, your resilience, and your light. When someone envies your very essence, they do not try to compete with you. They try to destroy you.

They envy your relationships, your peace, your potential, your faith, your reputation, and your inner strength. If you have survived pain, they cannot endure, they hate you for it. If you are still standing when they thought they crushed you, they become more dangerous.

The man I married resented everything about me that made me whole. He diminished my accomplishments. He tore down anything that made me feel proud or confident. He could not celebrate me because my light exposed his darkness.

Narcissistic envy is why they sabotage you. It is why they belittle you. It is why they withhold affection. It is why they smear your name. It is why they try to isolate you.

Deep down, they know they can not become like you, so they try to break you. When that does not work, they claim you are the envious one. It is a projection. It is madness. It is abuse.

To live with a narcissist is to walk on the fault line of their envy. Any moment of happiness, any ounce of attention you receive, any flicker of joy you experience is a threat to them. They become cold, bitter, or cruel. Your joy reminds them of everything they cannot feel.

"The narcissist wants to make sure you never feel good being you."

Narcissistic Regulation

Narcissistic regulation is the process by which a narcissist manages their outward behavior to protect their ego, avoid shame, and stay in control of their environment. These individuals do not regulate emotions like empathy, guilt, or sadness in the way emotionally healthy people do.

Instead, they regulate their image and the emotional climate around them. Their behavior shifts depending on who is present, what they want, or whether they feel their superiority is being questioned. In private, they may be cold, demeaning, or emotionally abusive, but if someone else enters the room, they can instantly become charming, attentive, or even loving. That dramatic shift is not confusion or instability, it is a calculated performance designed to protect their false self.

These shifts are not accidental. They are deliberate tactics used to maintain power and control. The narcissist may unleash rage when they feel criticized. They will retreat into silence when they cannot dominate a conversation. They will shower someone with affection when they sense their control is slipping. This is not an emotional connection; it is emotional manipulation. Narcissistic regulation allows them to shape the narrative, conceal the abuse, and confuse the victim, all while preserving their carefully crafted public image. To the outside world, they may appear calm and reasonable, but behind closed doors, they weaponize their behavior to keep their victim off balance, emotionally starved, and doubting their own reality.

Narcissistic Rage

Heinz Kohut, a psychoanalyst, coined the term "narcissistic rage." Narcissistic rage occurs on a continuum. It can range from aloofness or annoyance to serious outbursts and violent attacks. Narcissistic rage is a powerful and frightening emotional outburst triggered when the narcissist feels threatened, criticized, or exposed. It is not the normal anger most people experience; it is disproportionate, unpredictable, and often terrifying in its intensity. I have seen it many times. The facial expression changes instantly, revealing a look of pure hatred and deep-seated anger. It is as if the mask drops completely, and you are face-to-face with the raw hostility he works so hard to hide from the outside world.

This rage is not always loud. Sometimes it explodes in verbal assaults. Other times it is expressed through icy silence, calculated withdrawal, or passive-aggressive acts meant to punish and destabilize. In both forms, the intent is the same: to intimidate, control, and reassert dominance. The target is left feeling unsafe, confused, and hyper-alert, knowing that even the smallest perceived offense can ignite it again.

Living with narcissistic rage means living in a constant state of readiness, scanning for signs that the storm is about to break. It conditions the victim to tiptoe through daily life, silencing their own needs and truth to avoid triggering the fury that lies just beneath the surface. Over time, this erodes not only the victim's sense of safety but also their sense of self.

Message to Victims:

Narcissistic rage is not something to take lightly. It can escalate quickly and, in some cases, become physically dangerous. Do not ignore the signs. If you see the mask drop and that unmistakable look of hatred and anger appear, recognize it as a warning. This is not a moment to argue or try to reason with them. It is a moment to protect yourself. Prioritize your safety above all else, even if that means leaving the room, the house, or the relationship. Your life and well-being are worth far more than winning an argument with someone who thrives on conflict.

"Narcissistic rage can be dangerous. It should be viewed with caution."

Narcissistic Outsourcing

Outsourcing is one of the deceptive tools narcissists use. This is not about delegating, it is about avoiding accountability. It is how the narcissists keep their hands clean while making another person carry their emotional mess. When something goes wrong, the narcissists immediately look for someone else to blame. That is where the outsourcing begins.

They outsource:

- Blame – It is never their fault. It is always yours.

- Shame – They make you feel embarrassed for the very things they have done.

- Conflict – They send others to "talk to you" so they do not have to confront anything directly.

- Anger – You become the container for the rage they cannot face in themselves.

Sometimes, they even outsource their identity. They take on pieces of your personality, your values, your empathy until they have mirrored you so well that you forget where you end and they begin. I did not have a name for it at the time, but I lived it. The man I married did not just manipulate me; he made me responsible for his moods, his failures, his image, his lies. I was the one apologizing for things I did not do. I was the one fixing what he broke. That was outsourcing.

Looking back, I believe the man I married and I somehow exchanged identities. Over time, I absorbed his shame, his silence, his self-contempt. He adopted my strength, my voice, and my kindness as if they were his. That, too, was part of outsourcing. This tactic is especially damaging because it is quiet. It does not scream like rage. It whispers in gaslighting, in guilt trips, in forced silence. You do not realize it is happening. It is exhausting and confusing. You are constantly wondering why you feel so responsible.

Victims need to understand this:

You are not their emotional dumping ground.

You are not their scapegoat.

You are not responsible for what they refuse to carry.

Narcissistic Projection

Narcissistic outsourcing is about avoiding responsibility; narcissistic projection is about avoiding the truth of who they really are. It is a psychological defense mechanism commonly used by narcissists to protect their fragile self-esteem and avoid facing their own flaws, guilt, or insecurities. Instead of acknowledging their negative feelings or behaviors, narcissists project these onto others. This means they accuse others of having the traits, actions, or emotions that they themselves are struggling with or refusing to recognize.

A narcissist who feels intense jealousy might accuse their partner of being jealous, even though it IS not the partner's behavior that is in question. Similarly, a narcissist who lies frequently may accuse others of dishonesty. This projection keeps the narcissist from confronting their own shortcomings and redirects attention to their victim, further isolating and confusing them. Narcissists use projection as a way to maintain control in the relationship and shift blame. It is a tool that distorts reality, leaving the victim to question their own behavior, feel undeserving guilt, or second-guessing their perceptions.

If you are being projected upon, remember the accusations are not a reflection of who you are. Narcissists use projection to avoid facing their own flaws and manipulate your reality. Their criticism is not your burden. Trust yourself, know that their projections are about them, not you. You deserve to have your own truth, free from their distortions.

"The narcissist makes you carry his shadow while he wears your light."

Keeping The Narcissist Calm To Survive

The man I married and I returned to the house in Georgia. My friend had been painting inside. There were no beds, just two mats on the floor. We slept in the same room on separate mats. I said, This feels peaceful." I asked the man I married if he felt peaceful, as well; he agreed in the affirmative. I think we both felt peace for that brief moment in time. The silence did not feel threatening for that moment. My body felt relief.

In the morning, I went to church. I came home and made lunch for us. We sat in that same room and ate like two ordinary people. Something inside me shifted because I was aware this was not authentic. We were both performing. I needed space. I went to the garage, my place of genuine peace.

When I returned to the inside of the house, he did not say a word to me. He did not look at me. I felt the still coldness. I caught a quick glance at me. What I saw in that quick glance was pure hatred, it generated a feeling of fear. I felt it immediately. My body became nervous, unsettled. My heart picked up its pace, and my mind began to race. I knew this feeling. I had felt it many times before. His silence was not neutral; it was his weapon. I returned to the garage.

The man I married later came into the garage to take out the trash. He said he was going to the store. I asked if I could ride with him. I needed to get out of the house, to calm him down, and to calm myself. He quickly said yes. We went. The tension broke. It worked for both of us.

This is what it is like to live with a narcissist. You find yourself constantly trying to stabilize their moods, read their cues, adjust your behavior to avoid the next cold silence, the next act of contempt. It feels insane.

One moment you are sitting together peacefully, and the next you are being punished for something unspoken. There is always a feeling of threat in their silence, in their eyes, in the way your body responds before your brain can catch up. It is a constant struggle for survival.

Clarity

He told me I ruined vacations. He said I made things difficult. He said I was the reason everything went wrong. I believed him. I often thought, "Maybe I am the problem." I spent years trying to fix what I did not break, apologizing for things I did not do. Now I know the truth. He was not reacting to me. He was outsourcing his inner misery, his shame, his frustration, his unspoken failures.

He could not stand to feel those things, so he handed them to me. I was never the cause. I was the container. Clarity does not come all at once. It arrives in pieces, in flashbacks, in sudden understanding, in the sharp contrast between who you are and how you were treated. Once it comes, you can never go back. Clarity is the moment your healing begins, even if the pain still lingers. Once you know the truth, you stop carrying what never belonged to you.

For the woman who has been blamed for everything:

- *If he ruined the moment and told you it was your fault, it was not.*

- *If you spent years trying to fix things you did not break, it was never your job.*

- *If you believed his misery was because of you, it was not.*

- *If he handed you his shame and called it yours, it was not.*

A Deceptive Predator

There comes a terrifying moment when you finally see what and whom you have been living with. He is not a partner, not a protector; he is a predator. A predator who wears a charm mask and deception like a second skin.

You believed you were building a life together. You believed in his smile, his promises, his presence beside you. While all the time he was hunting for attention, for control, for supply. He could flirt with someone in front of you, a friend, or an associate. Then he would pretend it meant nothing. He could betray you in daylight, then gaslight you in the dark. You doubt yourself. You question your instincts. You make excuses for him, over and over. He makes you believe it is all in your head.

When the evidence becomes undeniable; when the mask starts to slip; something strange happens inside you; you experience **_cognitive dissonance._** You begin to live in two realities. One part of you sees the truth, the cruelty, the lies, the betrayal. The other part still clings to the version of him you believe in; the man you love, the man you need him to be. This psychological conflict is paralyzing. It keeps you stuck in confusion, hoping for a return to the fantasy and terrified of facing the truth. You begin to second-guess everything about the relationship.

I now recognize the man I married to be the deceptive predator that he has always been. He wore a mask so convincing that I believed it for decades. I have to be vigilant in my stance because cognitive dissonance can weaken one's resolve if you are not strong.

To The Women Reading This:

If you feel something is wrong, trust your instincts. If he makes you feel invisible, crazy, or unworthy, that is his goal. He wants to keep you confused and off balance. In that way, he maintains control and power over you. You are not imagining it. You are being conditioned to believe that you are the problem.

Please do not wait decades like I did.

Please do not spend your life trying to fix someone who never intended to love you.

Do not confuse crumbs with kindness. Do not mistake control for commitment.

You may not know what freedom looks like yet, but you do know what fear feels like.

When you recognize the predator, you become the woman who refuses to be his prey.

Strategic Survival

There is a moment in every survivor's journey when the fog begins to lift. What once felt like confusion becomes clarity. You no longer make excuses for their behavior. You no longer tell yourself it is just a bad day or a misunderstanding. You know who they are. That awareness changes everything.

Some leave the relationship. Others, like me, stay. We do not stay because we are weak. We do not stay because we are in denial. We stay because we are surviving strategically. We remain in the environment, but not in the illusion. We no longer seek love, validation, or repair. We no longer try to explain or defend. We stop playing the role they cast for us.

We may still live in the same house, eat at the same table, or even smile at the right times. But inside, we are disengaged, detached, and alert. We speak less. We react less. We observe. We preserve our energy. We measure our words. We manage the risk. We endure not with blind hope, but with awareness.

This kind of survival is not passivity. It is resistance. It is an emotional armor. It is what many women do when there is no safe exit, no financial lifeline, and no support from the outside world. It is what we do when we finally see the truth and have to live with it every day. The danger becomes more real once we know. Before awareness, we felt only sadness or confusion. With awareness, we feel the threat. The narcissist often senses the shift. He sees that the mask no longer works. He will escalate, becoming more controlling, more paranoid, more cruel. He will begin a smear campaign. He will try to provoke breakdowns. He might seek revenge. The threat is no longer just emotional, it can be financial, social, or even physical. Strategic survival is not the end of your story, it is the beginning of reclaiming your life.

Guard your peace. Hold your boundaries. Document what matters. Speak only when necessary. Build support where you can. Protect your future. Above all, do not let the silence fool you, he is still who he always was.

If you are still there because of money, fear, age, shame, or uncertainty, know that I see you. I am 78 years old. I understand what it means to stay, even after knowing. I am not writing this from a place of judgment; I am writing this because I have lived it. I am living it.

Every day that you keep your spirit alive is a quiet victory. Every day that you maintain your clarity is an act of power. Every day that you survive with your eyes open is resistance. This is strategic survival. It is real.

Psychological Abuse

Psychological abuse is a form of abuse characterized by a person subjecting or exposing another person to a behavior that may result in trauma, anxiety, depression, stress, and other psychological problems.

The man I married is not a physical abuser. His physical abuse can be triggered by something that I say or something that I do, causing injury to his ego. I recall only four times in five decades when there was physical abuse. He once became enraged and pushed me against a wall during the early months of my pregnancy. He once became enraged and knocked me to the concrete garage floor during our early years of marriage. He once became enraged and tackled me to the floor in our current home. He once became enraged and threw objects at me at our current home. His abuse is psychological. It plays havoc with me mentally and emotionally. In a psychologically abusive relationship, one person exerts power over another person. Psychological abuse is difficult to recognize and difficult to prove.

There are no easily recognizable wounds on display for others to see. Psychological abuse causes wounds that are embedded internally, where they cannot be seen. It is where there is bleeding of the wounds to the soul, a place impossible for others to see. These internal wounds cause massive damage to the body, mind, and soul.

Psychological abuse generates a constant state of guilt, self-doubt, fear, insecurity, confusion, uncertainty, and anxiety. I have and continue to experience these emotions because I remain in a narcissistic, abusive relationship. Psychological abuse is a brutally cruel form of abuse perpetrated by a narcissist. The effects are long-term; recovery is difficult.

Psychological Abuser

The psychological abuser uses tactics like deflection, projection, and gaslighting. The psychological abuser's purpose is to keep the victim off balance and under control.

The psychological abuser deflects their bad behaviors onto the victim, makes the victim feel guilty, and blames the victim for what the abuser has actually done. The victim apologizes to the abuser, unknowingly assuming blame for something that they did not do. It is cruel and devastating.

The psychological abuser projects negative feelings and thoughts onto the victim. The abuser says the victim is jealous, is insecure, or is insane. This is indicative of the feelings the abuser has about self. It is destructive to the victim.

The psychological abuser gaslights the victim. The abuser strives to make the victim believe false versions of events when the victim has precise remembrances of said events. It traumatizes the victim's mind, leading to a destination of devastation and destruction.

The psychological abuser uses these tactics repeatedly over time with precision. The victim is left confused and traumatized. The victim is ultimately perceived as the unstable one in the relationship. The abuser is seen as stable and caring.

The psychological abuser is the narcissist in your life who lurks behind the mask of deception.

Action	Description
Isolating	Blaming
Name-calling	Excluding
Denying	Rejecting
Threatening	Ignoring
Humiliating	Withholding

These are all actions I have been subjected to throughout the decades of being with the man I married. His actions have resulted in devastation and destruction to my mind, my body, and my soul. I am desperately seeking the recovery that remains out of reach.

Cognitive Empathy Vs. Emotional Empathy

In my experience with narcissistic abuse, I have come to understand the difference between cognitive empathy and emotional empathy and how this distinction has shaped my pain.

Cognitive Empathy is the ability to understand someone's feelings or thoughts, but it does not require emotional involvement. The man I married has shown cognitive empathy countless times. He knows exactly when I am upset or hurt, but his understanding has always been detached and manipulative. He uses that knowledge to control or gaslight me, but never with genuine care.

Emotional Empathy, on the other hand, is about feeling someone else's emotions, truly sharing in their pain. This is something the man I married lacks. He may know my pain, but he does not feel it. His responses are cold, calculated, and performative, leaving me feeling emotionally isolated and unsupported.

For years, I believed that because he understood my emotions, he must care. But the truth is, he only knew how to manipulate my feelings, not connect with them. His cognitive empathy was used as a tool to control, never to heal.

This imbalance between understanding and feeling has been one of the most damaging aspects of our relationship, leaving me questioning if he ever truly cared at all.

To Other Women:

If you find yourself in a relationship where your pain is understood, but never truly felt, you deserve a partner who not only recognizes your emotions but also connects with them.

You deserve someone who responds with genuine care, not manipulation. You are not alone in this struggle. Know that your feelings matter.

Emotional-Detachment

Emotional detachment is a psychological state in which a person is unwilling or unable to form emotional connections with others. It is not always obvious on the surface, but beneath the calm or charming exterior, there is often a complete absence of empathy, affection, and emotional expressions.

In narcissistic individuals, emotional detachment is a core characteristic that causes profound damage to those closest to them. The victim is left confused, aching for warmth, and constantly questioning why the person they love remains so cold and indifferent. The longing becomes a torment. The smallest act of kindness or recognition becomes something the victim desperately clings to.

This has been my unfortunate experience for decades with the man I married. I gave everything to him. I gave him my time, my love, my body, and my strength. I desperately wanted to be seen, to be heard, and to be loved by the man I married; but all of it was in vain. I now know I was pouring it all into an emotional void, a place where love did not exist. It was a place that lacked compassion and genuine connection. The sad truth is, the man I married emotionally detached from me a long time ago. To him, I was not a human being to be love; I was an object to be controlled, used, devalued, discarded, trashed, and replaced at his whim.

His emotional detachment did not just hurt me. It devastated me. It destroyed who I was. And yet, I have stayed. For a long time, I hoped I could still reach him. I hoped he might change. I hoped I might matter.

The truth is: Emotional detachment, in the hands of the man I married, is not indifference. It is a weapon and I am its target.

Trauma

Von Der Kolk is a renowned psychiatrist who has done extensive studies and research on trauma. According to him, trauma is an event that overwhelms the central nervous system, causing an altering to the way people process and recall memories. He states, "Trauma is not the story of something that happened back then; it is the current imprint of that pain and fear inside of people".

The trauma victims experience in narcissistic relationships becomes stored deeply inside the body. Stored trauma generates pain and progressively destroys the health of the body and the mind.

Trauma Common Side Effects

- Rumination

- Flashbacks

- Nightmares

- Intrusive thoughts

- Intense stress and distress

- Physical sensations and ailments

- Suicide ideation

All of these side effects of trauma and betrayal, I testify to be true. I experience all of them. They impact the quality of my life. There are no medications that will counteract these side effects. The body struggles to endure on its own accord.

Betrayal Trauma

Jennifer Freyd, an American psychologist, introduced the concept of betrayal trauma. Betrayal trauma occurs when the people a person relies on for protection, resources, and survival violate the trust or well-being of that person. Betrayal trauma occurs often in narcissistic relationships. It is a side effect that develops when a victim learns about a trusted partner's lies, deceit, and infidelities. Betrayal trauma is devastatingly painful for the victim. This type of trauma challenges the victim's sense of

self-worth. It affects how the victim sees self and the people in the world around them. Many victims of trauma betrayal go through several common stages.

Side Effect	Side Effect
Negative thoughts	Suicide ideations
Hopelessness	Depression
Anxiety	Panic attacks
Avoidance	Trust issues

Hyper-vigilance	Mental anguish
Loss of appetite	Sleep disturbances

These side effects negatively affect the body, mind, and soul of victims who struggle with the perils of narcissistic abuse. I can relate so well to all of these side effects. I have the experience of five decades struggling to cope with them. They deprive me of peace, happiness, and joy in my life. I am lost in a never-ending cycle that spins continuously.

The Weight of Betrayal Trauma

Betrayal trauma does not leave clean wounds. It hides in the subtle moments. Something feels off, but you can not explain why. It lingers in the gut instinct that whispers, *something is not right,* and in the words you are given to silence that instinct.

On Hilton Head Island, there was a woman. He told me about her often. Said she was just a friend. Said he was helping her. Said it was nothing. But the way he spoke of her so frequently and so carefully left me uneasy. It was not what he said. It was what I *felt.* That feeling that something was being hidden in plain sight. He denied anything improper. Laughed off the idea. Dismissed me as jealous, suspicious, and paranoid. There is the recurring dream: *"I loved her,"* he whispers in my sleep. I wake to physical and mental anguish.

This is betrayal trauma: When your heart knows something your mind can not prove, when you are made to feel unstable for noticing the cracks in the story. When your pain is dismissed while the lies are protected, I still ruminate. Not because I want to, but because the door was never closed. I was never given the truth. I was left to carry the weight alone.

And still, I rise like a wounded warrior.

Trauma Physiology

Trauma physiology is how the body stores and responds to trauma long after the threat is gone. When the nervous system remains in a constant state of alert, the body does not calm down. It becomes hyper-vigilant.

 When I am in the presence of the man I married, oftentimes my vision blurs, my chest tightens, my legs ache. I feel on the verge of a panic attack. This is not a weakness. My body is remembering. My nervous system learned to detect danger before I could verbalize what was happening. When you live for decades with emotional abuse, the body is always on guard.

For victims of narcissistic abuse, trauma physiology is the silent, invisible proof that something is wrong. It is the body's way of protecting when no one else will.

Trauma Patterns

I often ask myself, *Why did I end up in such a toxic, abusive relationship?* The answer, I believe, lies in my early childhood. My grandmother was distant, cold, and controlling. Her emotional absence left me craving approval and fearing rejection.

I became skilled at suppressing my own needs to avoid punishment or disapproval. I was taught to be quiet; to be good, to be tolerate, to endure. That became a pattern; a conditioned way of surviving.

So when I met the man I married, I poured all of myself into him. When he withdrew, I reached harder. When he gave little, I gave more. I begged to be acknowledged, to be seen, to matter. I did not question. I adapted. I stayed. It felt *familiar*. I was loyal to people who were never loyal to me. I did not realize I was functioning from trauma conditioning patterns I did not choose. They evolved from the wounds of my childhood. When you finally see those trauma patterns clearly, you begin to understand. It was never a weakness. It was survival. Awareness is the beginning of freedom. Only when you recognize the patterns can you begin to break them and become who you truly are.

Why Victims Stay

Some friends who read my book, "Lurking Behind the Mask," asked, "Why didn't you just leave?"

The answer will be different for each individual circumstance, however, there are some commonalities.

Many victims of narcissistic abuse have low self-esteem; we doubt ourselves. We become experts at surviving, not living. We stay because we are committed to family. We stay because we are bound financially. We stay because we fear the losses. We stay even as it slowly kills us.

I desperately clung to hope that things would change; that life would get better. We moved several times to different states. My anticipation was that life would be better in a new environment; it never was. It worsened like the tormented life I experienced on Hilton Head Island.

What people need to understand is that victims of narcissistic abuse get trapped. We are trapped in an invisible cage called a trauma bond. It is a bond that silences your pain and binds the heart to someone who harms you.

The Trauma Bond

A trauma bond is an emotional attachment that develops between a person and an abuser. For victims of narcissistic abuse, the trauma bond formed is like a powerful addiction. Once established, it is very difficult to break.

The trauma bond I had with my maternal grandmother existed for years after I moved away from her influence over my life. The bond was finally broken when she died.

The trauma bond between the narcissist and the victim develops subtly. It slowly progresses over time without the victim's awareness that it is happening. The victim gets boxed in, not realizing how they got trapped.

The narcissist methodically feeds the victim all the craving good stuff. The narcissist generously disperses love, attention, and intimacy. Then, without warning, the narcissist changes the meal plan. The narcissist disperses anger, criticism, and rejection. This becomes a repeated pattern. The victim is boxed into a perpetual state of confusion, anxiety, and hunger. Hunger for the good stuff that only comes at the whim of the narcissist.

The trauma bond I had to the man I married persisted for decades. It kept me tightly tethered to him. I could not envision life without him. I loved him more than I loved myself. It disgusts me to make such defacing admissions; it is my unfortunate truth.

The trauma bond is extremely difficult to break. It was a challenge for me to break away from my maternal grandmother so many years ago. The man I married was a very powerful addiction. It was the challenge of a lifetime to break the bond with him. In time, through knowledge, through meditation, and through prayer, I was able to break it. It was a feeling of liberation from bondage. There was no longer any need for validation from the man I married. I was free to be me.

He was the love of my life for over five decades, but he is no longer that love in the present times. Today, he is merely my family. I care about him and his welfare because he is the family member with whom I have shared most of my life. It deeply saddens me to know that his feelings for me are not reciprocal. That is just the fact of life I must accept. There is no way to change his lack of genuine feelings for me and my well-being. He is a narcissist; my time with him has exceeded beyond its expiration date. In his delusional mind, my existence is doomed to the trash. That is my devastating truth. The pain is destroying me mentally and physically. I am struggling for survival.

I am confident the cords that kept me tethered to the man I married for over five decades have finally been severed. I still have my weak moments, but I am no longer living the fantasy he created; I am living the reality that exists. I am able to distinguish between the two.

Intermittent Reinforcement

Intermittent reinforcement refers to a reinforcement schedule in which a desired behavior is rewarded only occasionally and never consistently. B.F. Skinner, an American psychologist and behaviorist, is credited with the development of intermittent reinforcement.

According to Skinner, people can be conditioned to react to rewards and punishments. Intermittent reinforcement is commonly seen in narcissistic, abusive relationships. The victim becomes conditioned to the ups and downs of the relationship. Sometimes the narcissist is kind and loving; other times the narcissist is cruel and neglectful. The victim gets stuck in this pattern of behavior, never knowing what to expect, but always anticipating and hoping for the kindness and love to come from the narcissist. Intermittent reinforcement leads to the development of a victim's trauma bond to the narcissistic abuser.

Rumination

One of the most damaging ways trauma continues to harm us long after the events have passed is through rumination. Rumination is the mental replay of painful events, conversations, or imagined scenarios over and over again. It is like a record that keeps skipping back to the same point, never moving forward. For survivors of narcissistic abuse, rumination becomes a constant loop, analyzing what was said, wondering why it happened, and imagining how it could have been different.

It is the brain's attempt to make sense of the senseless. When you have been lied to, gaslit, and emotionally attacked, your mind searches for meaning and clarity that may never come. The problem is, rumination does not bring closure. It deepens the wound, prolongs emotional pain, and delays healing.

Narcissists thrive when their victims are trapped in rumination because it keeps the focus on them, even when they are absent. Breaking the cycle takes conscious effort: redirecting thoughts, focusing on the present moment, and reminding yourself that you cannot rewrite the past, only reclaim your future.

Message To Those Stuck In Rumination

If you are trapped in replaying the pain, know this: you are not weak, broken, or failing. Your mind is searching for answers that may never come. The past will not change, no matter how many times you revisit it. Each time you break the loop, you take back a piece of yourself. Freedom begins in the moment you decide to live in today, not yesterday.

The Hidden Damage

Narcissistic abuse does not leave visible bruises, but it scars the mind and body in ways that are just as real and just as devastating. I spent decades living in emotional chaos. Behind closed doors, I was gaslit, devalued, and isolated. The stress of feeling unsafe emotionally and mentally took root inside me and became my normal.

Over time, I began to unravel. I did not realize it then, but my mind and body were breaking under the weight of psychological abuse. I was diagnosed with major depression and anxiety/panic disorder. For over 30 years, I saw psychiatrists. I took medication not to thrive, but to function and to survive as I continued to live in the fog that narcissistic abuse creates.

Victims of this kind of abuse often suffer in silence. The outside world sees a calm face, but inside, we are drowning.

Narcissistic abuse can lead to:

- Chronic anxiety

- Depression

- Insomnia

- Memory loss or confusion

- Panic attacks

- Hyper-vigilance (constantly feeling on edge)

- Physical pain with no clear medical cause

These symptoms are real. They are not imagined. They are the body's way of responding to prolonged emotional trauma. Some professionals call it Complex PTSD, a condition caused by repeated abuse over time, especially when the abuser is someone you love or depend on.

I lived this reality. I am still living with its aftermath. I may never be completely healed, but I know now: **"I was never crazy."** What happened to me was real. It left damage that cannot be seen and must never be denied.

Complex PTSD(C-PTSD)

I did not know there was a name for what I feel. I just know I am in unrelenting pain; a kind of pain that never ceases to be. A pain that lives in my body, in my thoughts, in the way I see the world.

That name is **Complex PTSD.**

C-PTSD does not come from one traumatic event; it comes from prolonged, repeated abuse. It is what happens when you are gaslit, silenced, controlled, manipulated, neglected, and dehumanized for years or, like me, for decades. I was told I was the problem. I was made to feel like I was crazy, dramatic, and unstable.

I was being emotionally and psychologically abused in ways that the public does not see. I had no explanation for what was happening to me.

C-PTSD showed up in me as:

- Emotional flashbacks and nightmares

- Anxiety and panic attacks

- Constant fear of being wrong, of being rejected, of being abandoned

- Persistent need to please, to appease, to never make mistakes

- Unrelenting pain in the body and in the mind.

I did not feel safe in my own home for decades, always fearful and always anxious. To the world outside my home, I appeared fine. No one noticed that I was drowning in fear, pain, and anxiety. **That is the reality of someone experiencing C-PTSD. If you dare to share these feelings, you are labeled unstable.**

The Devastation And Destruction Of Narcissistic Abuse

Narcissistic abuse is not just emotional mistreatment, it is psychological warfare. It steals your clarity, erodes your voice, and breaks down your sense of self. The person who once claimed to love you becomes the architect of your emotional ruin. The damage is slow, silent, and often invisible. It is real and it is devastating.

It does not strike all at once. It creeps in quietly through charm, through false affection, through promises that feel like love, but are weapons in disguise. It begins with confusion. Then comes self-doubt. Then the slow, brutal unraveling of everything you thought you knew.

You become a stranger to yourself. You speak, but you are not heard. You exist, but you are not seen. You are alive, but you do not feel like you are living. The abuse takes root in your nervous system. It haunts your sleepless nights. It buries your confidence and poisons your sense of reality.

The most unbearable part is not just the pain; it is the betrayal of believing it was love. The narcissist creates a world where you question your sanity, doubt your worth, and beg for the very thing that is destroying you. Somehow, you believe that if you were just better, more forgiving, more patient, more silent, the abuse might stop. It does not stop because hurting you is how they maintain control.

The narcissist wears a mask so polished that others applaud the performance, while you are left bleeding behind closed doors. The world sees kindness. You endure cruelty. The narcissist is adored. You are dismissed, disbelieved, and discarded.

The long-term effects of narcissistic abuse stretch far beyond the immediate trauma.

The emotional and psychological damage lingers, often manifesting as Complex PTSD (CPTSD). Survivors experience chronic anxiety, panic attacks, and deep depression. Emotional numbness becomes a defense mechanism, and the isolation that the abuse fosters can create a sense of being completely alone, even in a crowded room.

The toll on the body is equally profound. The stress from constant manipulation and control wears down your immune system, leaving you vulnerable to illness. Chronic headaches, gastrointestinal issues, and unexplained pain become regular parts of life. The inability to sleep, coupled with heightened stress, leads to exhaustion and fatigue that never seems to subside. Your body, like your mind, becomes a battlefield. The constant emotional upheaval keeps you on edge, triggering physical symptoms that only add to the emotional weight you carry.

I have personally lived through much of this, experiencing the anxiety, the emotional detachment, and the physical toll of living in a constant state of fear. Chronic pain, digestive issues, and sleepless nights have been the result of years of stress and emotional abuse. The invisible scars of narcissistic abuse do not fade. They are carried with you, and their impact is felt in ways that no one can see.

These long-term effects are not just collateral damage; they are the reality for those who live in the shadow of a narcissist. The damage is slow, but it is real, and it is lasting.

Living in an Alternate Reality

After the devastation and destruction, something even more cruel remains:

You find yourself existing in an *alternate state of reality*; a world that no one else can see or understand. This is the secret terrain where narcissistic abuse places you. It is not just emotional damage, it is disconnection from your own life. You are awake, but nothing feels real. You are breathing, but you do not feel alive. Other people live in the real world. You walk among them, but you are no longer part of them. Even those who once loved you now look through you, or worse, believe the lies told *about* you.

This exile is not metaphorical. It is the psychological space where trauma, gaslighting, and betrayal send you. It is where reality bends and trust evaporates. It is where you scream into empty rooms and beg the silence to answer you. You are not crazy. You are surviving in a world that was carefully built to keep you questioning yourself.

You are surviving the unseeable. The deepest wound is the loss of those you love, especially your child, your precious son. That fracture is irreparable. It is the cruelest twist in this altered reality. They believe the abuser. They reject you.

This is not a chapter in a story, it is a state of being. A parallel existence where survivors of narcissistic abuse are left to wander, searching for pieces of themselves that were taken, scattered, and buried beneath a lifetime of abuse and trauma.

This is not an exaggeration. It is not drama. It is the lived experience of countless victims who are left traumatized, gaslit, and broken.

If you are reading this and wondering whether your pain has a name, it does. Narcissistic abuse is a theft of identity. It is the destruction of dignity. It is a slow, calculated devastation of the self.

This book is not about healing; it is about surviving what was designed to destroy me. Narcissistic abuse does not just hurt: It devastates. It destroys. It is, without question, *A Destination to Devastation and Destruction.*

Coping Mechanisms

I tolerated 51 years of abuse before I realized I was trapped inside a bubble. A bubble especially created for me by a covert narcissist, the man I loved and married. Trapped inside this bubble, I experienced the narcissistic cycles of idealization, devaluation, and discard over and over. There was no ending for me. He was slowly devastating and destroying the essence of me. I knew something was dreadfully wrong as I remained lost in a maze of confusion for five decades.

One day, a higher power stepped forth and pierced a hole in that bubble my abuser assumed to be impenetrable. It happened when the man I married most brutally and cruelly discarded me. He went into a no contact mode with me for three tormenting weeks. Never in five decades had I been separated from him with no contact. I experienced all the effects of trauma and betrayal.

I had negative thoughts, hopelessness, anxiety, nightmares, depression, and panic attacks. I could not sleep, and I could not eat. I was a total wreck. However, through all that trauma, the warrior in me did not allow me to reach out to him. I was hurting so badly, but my pride would not let me cave. I suffered silently as I waited for him to return.

When I emerged from that bubble, I was unstable, broken, and gasping for air. A higher power helped me, guided me, and gave me the willpower to survive. I had the determination of a wounded warrior who would not succumb to defeat. I rose up from the depths of despair to ascend to a higher plane where I sought knowledge and discovery. I had an insatiable appetite to educate myself on the facets of narcissism and narcissistic abuse.

"Education is the avenue to discovery and understanding. It is a shield of protection providing tools of defense."

DR. RAMANI

Dr. Ramani is an outspoken advocate for victims of narcissistic abuse. She is a clinical psychologist and an expert on all things narcissistic. Dr. Ramani is passionate about helping victims of narcissistic abuse. She is empathetic, and she understands the plight of victims of narcissistic abuse.

In her videos, she provides strategies and promotes recovery for victims. She has written many books on narcissism and has made many videos. I watched numerous videos made by Dr. Ramani in the past two years. I listened attentively to what she said. It took two years for me to absorb and to finally understand what she was conveying. It took two years because I remained stagnant. I was hoping that somehow my situation with the man I married could be the rare exception. I erroneously thought I would get through to him. I erroneously thought some human understanding would come from him. I erroneously hoped for some caring emotions to spring forth from him. My hopes were all in vain because the man I married did not have the capability to do any of that. He did not care about my needs and my wants. His needs and wants were and are the only ones that matter in his world; the world where I resided with him for five decades.

Dr. Ramani defines and clarifies the behaviors of a narcissistic person. Narcissists do not hear you when you express your feelings. Narcissists do not have the capacity to care about you nor your feelings. Your engagement with them fuels their ego. Your engagement is the sustenance for their survival. Your engagement can be negative or positive. It does not make any difference. Your engagement is their stimulus for power and control. Control and power confirm their existence in the world. During those two years, I attempted to engage with the man I married over and over again. I expressed my feelings verbally. I cried constantly and yearned for some expression of love from him. I craved for some recognition of my existence. His response was either an enraged outburst, stone-cold heartlessness, or silence. He only spoke to me when it was beneficial to him. My efforts were all to no avail. I wasted my time and my energy.

I disrespected myself by bowing down to the master like a slave. It was exactly as Dr. Ramani emphasized in the videos I watched. It finally registered in my foggy mind after two years of desperately trying to have a human connection with the man I married. The pain and the struggle are indescribable.

DR. LES CARTER

Dr. Les Carter is a clinical psychotherapist and a leading expert on narcissism. He has many informative and help videos on narcissism.

He is a great advocate for narcissistic abuse survivors. I watched many of his videos and have learned much from him.

LEE HAMMOCK

Lee Hammock is a self-aware, diagnosed narcissist. According to Lee, his goal is to raise awareness about NPD, narcissistic personality disorder. Lee is a strong advocate for victims of narcissistic abuse. He shares stories from his past. He presents strategies for victims to use to protect themselves from the devastation and destruction of narcissistic abuse. A direct quote from Lee, "If they can trigger you, they can control you." I know from experience, this is a profound truth.

I have listened to numerous videos by Lee Hammock. His insights have been invaluable to me. The knowledge that comes from him is mighty and enlightening.

LEON WALKER

Leon Walker is a diagnosed self aware narcissist. According to Leon, his objective is to give people a deep insight into narcissism. He has many insightful videos available. He reveals the mindset of a person with NPD. In many of the videos he shares, he describes the narcissistic behaviors he exhibited in relationships with women before he became self-aware of his narcissism. He acknowledges that men and women who have NPD are cheaters and manipulators. He is a great source for gathering knowledge about narcissism and narcissistic abuse.

OPRAH WINFREY AND DENZEL WASHINGTON

There are well-known celebrities who are now voicing their thoughts and insights regarding narcissism and narcissistic abuse.

Oprah Winfrey and Denzel Washington offer informative and motivational podcasts on narcissism and narcissistic abuse. I listen attentively and absorb their messages. They advocate for victims of narcissistic abuse. I listen to them repeatedly. I especially listen in moments when I feel weak, doubtful, and vulnerable. They inspire me and keep me grounded.

"CIRCLES"

I joined an online support group called "Circles." The groups are composed of many men and women who are survivors of narcissistic abuse. Professionals facilitate the groups. You can listen to others' stories, and you can share yours. You can join group sessions anytime during the day or night. It is the cheapest therapy you can find that really provides help to people going through the agonizing effects of narcissistic abuse.

The "Circles" groups have helped me through some of my darkest days. It is an online app that I strongly recommend. You will find many supportive professionals and narcissistic survivors who hear you and understand your pain. I have interacted with people all across the United States. We all share similar stories of narcissistic abuse. It is an immense feeling of relief to converse with people who totally understand the struggles and the pain of narcissistic abuse.

Hatred

Hatred is a deep-seated and intense emotional dislike or aversion towards something; it comes with feelings of anger, contempt, and disgust. When a victim of narcissistic abuse is liberated from the boxed trap of the narcissist and asserts autonomy, there is a shift in the dynamics of the relationship between the victim and narcissist.

The victim awakens and becomes cognizant. The victim recognizes the narcissist's devastating and destructive tactics. The victim begins to regain power. The narcissist senses the shift. The narcissist intensifies the tactics that always worked in the past.

The narcissist incorporates desperate measures to regain the power and the control once held over the victim. This is when the victim sees the true "self" of the narcissist who lurks behind the mask.

Maya Angelou, a renowned poet, is often quoted:

"When someone shows you who they are, believe them the first time."

The cruel actions of the narcissist exude hatred for the victim. The victim hears the hatred in the sarcastic tone of the narcissist's voice. The victim feels the hatred expressed in the cutting words of the narcissist. The victim internalizes the hatred experienced from the actions of the narcissist. The narcissist's hatred is palpable.

I live in a home with a man who exudes hatred like a caustic fume that is corrosive to my mind, my body, my soul. His tone is sarcastic. His speech is hurtful. His actions are fearful. He rejects me. He ignores me. I breathe his caustic fumes of hatred. His hatred evokes a life-threatening choke. How long can I remain alive in this toxic abuse?

During one of the man I married's enraged outbursts:

He shouted at me, "Eat shit and die!"

It echoes in my ears.

It ruminates in my mind.

It aches in my heart.

It wounds in my soul.

That is hatred spoken clarity.

That is recovery impossibility.

That is devastation and destruction.

I see the man I married so differently now that I am out of the fog. I am plagued by the fact that I did not know. I had no clue as to his true character. This man was my world. He was my reason for living. I loved him. I adored him. In my world, he reigned omnipotent. Perhaps that was my sin. Perhaps my pain and suffering are justifiable punishment for my sin. Hatred does not always explode. Sometimes, it simmers. It watches. It waits. It can be a quiet threat that lingers in silence.

Now that I see clearly and he knows I see, something has shifted. I do not believe he wants what is best for me. I believe he wants me quiet, gone, forgotten. The fear is not imagined; it is the voice of the body protecting you. Fear is my companion. It moves with me through the day and follows me into the night. Fear lives inside me quietly and constantly. I never feel safe.

This is the kind of fear so many victims of narcissistic abuse live with. The fear of being punished for waking up. The fear that truth has made us dangerous simply because we revealed it.

"These days, when the man I married looks at me, his facial expression displays pure hatred.

That expression devastates me and destroys me; it murders my soul."

Contempt

Contempt is colder than hatred. It does not explode; it dismisses. It sends the message:

- You are not worth my time.
- You are beneath me.
- Your feelings do not matter.
- I will erase you without ever raising my voice.

The man I married often shows contempt in cutting ways, the sarcastic tone, the looks that say, *"You are nothing."* He does not have to raise his voice. His silence is enough. His smirks are enough. His expressions of disgust are enough. His disdain pierces deeper than any insult.

The narcissist feels contempt not because of who *you* are, but because of what you represent to *him*. Your strength, your pain, your survival, your refusal to fully disappear, these things expose what he tries to hide from the world and himself.

"The narcissist's contempt is never a reflection of your worth. It is a reflection of his emptiness."

Punished For Loving Him

He hates me. Not for harm I have done, but for the light I carry.

His hatred whispers in silence, in eyes that look through me, in doors that close without a word.

Then it speaks, "I despise you." "I hate you."

This is not anger. This is contempt.

It is cold, calculated, and complete.

Somehow, it is mine to bear. My kindness offends him. My loyalty disgusts him. My presence reminds him of everything he is not.

He hates me because I see through him. He hates me because I refuse to disappear. He hates me because I still exist with a heart he cannot feel and a soul he cannot touch.

To the woman reading this with tears and a broken heart:

You are not hated because you are broken.

You are hated because you are whole.

You are not despised because you are weak.

You are despised because you still shine.

Your light terrifies the darkness.

I Believe He Always Hated Me

After years of silence, contempt, and cold withdrawal, I no longer ask myself if his feelings changed somewhere along the way. I have stopped trying to pinpoint when the shift happened because I believe it never did. I believe he always hated me. It was a quiet, bitter, hidden kind of hatred. The kind that lives beneath polite smiles, beneath normal conversations, beneath decades of shared space that felt like captivity instead of connection.

Even in the early years, when I thought we were building a life, something inside him resisted me. He tolerated me, used me, relied on me, but he did not *cherish* me. There was no warmth and true partnership. There was just resentment that deepened as I tried to love him into loving me back.

I think he hated me for needing him, trusting him, for surviving what he threw at me. It took me decades to see it. But now, it is clear.

There was no turning point because the hatred was always there. It was there the day I said, "I do." The day I embarked on a destination to devastation and destruction.

Does Minus Me Equal Happiness?

He has not left, but I feel the subtraction. I see the way he fades; how his presence dims; how his silence stretches wider each day.

I gave him everything. He gives me coldness and the ache of being erased in slow motion.

His body is here.

His mind is gone.

His eyes scan the distance for someone softer.

There is always someone waiting; someone who does not know the cost of standing where I stand.

One day, he will walk away smiling. He will give her the best of him; the mask he wore when I still believed. I will be the sum of what he left behind.

To the women sitting quietly in subtraction:

You are not the problem he is solving.

You are part of the equation he could never carry.

The happiness he finds without you will never add up to truth.

My Journals 2024 -2025

Journaling has been a vital aspect of my survival for the past year. When there was no one to talk with, writing soothed my mind, body, and soul. I share a selection of my journals because I want others to hear the depth of pain endured when one chooses to remain in a toxic narcissistic relationship. There is no peace. There is no joy. There is no happiness.

There is no hope. I want others to understand the emotional drain and unyielding heartache experienced hour after hour, day after day, week after week, month after month. It is incessant; there is no end in sight. It is painful, mental, and physical exhaustion. I am plagued by fear, anxiety, confusion, and uncertainty. I breathe, but I do not feel alive.

MY VOICED OPINION

May 26, 2024

Today is Sunday, May 26, 2024. The man I married and I had an argument. I voiced my opinion on a situation. He became enraged, saying I am crazy and insane. He left going to our son's house and stayed for hours. It is so peaceful being here alone. I am sitting on the deck, enjoying, listening, and sometimes dancing to music.

The man I married usually comes out and sits while I am out here. However, when he returned, he did not come out to where I am. I am feeling uncomfortable about his behavior at this point. I do not feel safe. I believe the man I married is potentially dangerous; he is capable of harming me. He hates me; my body feels his hatred; my ears hear his hatred. I live in fear in my home.

Veronica

FEAR

June 2, 2024

It is Sunday night, June 2, 2024. I don't feel safe. I fear that the man I married and our son might be plotting something behind my back. The man I married told me our son has read my book. He said our son is mad that I wrote the book. I was hoping our son could have a change of heart after reading my truth about his father's decades of abuse.

However, it seems our son supports his father. To me, that is an indication that our son might be narcissistic, as well. I believe a healthy-minded son would express some empathy for his mother, knowing she was abused for decades. My son has no empathy for me.

 I pray for a wall of protection.

Veronica

I AM HUMAN

July 18, 2024

Today is Thursday, July 18, 2024. The man I married and our son just had a long phone conversation. They talked about the grandchildren. They discussed their mutual health issues. I am sitting in the room, and neither of them acknowledges my presence. I wonder what kind of men they are. I am a human with feelings and emotions. They ignore me as if I do not exist. Lord, how is this possible! The man I married sits there all smug without a care in the world.

My life does not matter to these people. I cannot comprehend this world I live in; it is destroying me. I am trapped here with this unstable man. Nobody knows the truth but me. He wears the deceptive mask for the public.

Pray for me.

Veronica

PANIC ATTACK

July 24, 2024

Today is Wednesday, July 24, 2024. The man I married and I went to visit his uncle at the hospital today. There were four of us in the room, the man I married, his uncle, and his uncle's wife. This was his circle. I felt so detached from them.

I did not engage in conversation with them. The wife asked if I was okay. My response was, "No, I am not okay."

Her response was, "Well, you need to do something about that." She also said I should go back to taking my medications. Who says that to a person! She has read my book about narcissistic abuse. She read about the trauma I have endured for decades, and that is what she said to me; cold-hearted.

I did not feel comfortable sitting among the three of them.

When the man I married and I returned to the car, I began to have chest pains. I feared I was having a heart attack. I did not tell the man I married that I was experiencing chest pains. I began applying a tapping technique I learned.

I began repeating, "I am okay" silently. I also did some deep breathing. We stopped at a grocery store. While inside the store, I began to feel panicky and off balance. I fled from the store and rushed back to the car. I convinced myself it was a mere panic attack. I knew the symptoms well; I had multiple panic attacks during my marriage. I told myself I was safe; I was okay. I do not need to be in the presence of people whom I do not trust.

God, please protect me from harmful people.

Veronica

TRIGGERED

July 31, 2024

I started watching the movie, "Fatal Attraction." It triggered me to the point where I baited the man I married about his infidelities during our marriage. He became enraged and said hurtful things. I know I was wrong to bait him. It just gives me some relief when I confront him about the awful things he has done during our decades of marriage. I am disgusted with myself.

My friend and neighbor died suddenly on Sunday. I am grieving the loss of a dear friend. In his rage, the man I married said hurtful things about my deceased friend. He said he had discussions with her about me. He said my friend believed there was something wrong with me. This is the same tale he has told me about another deceased friend of mine. This is typical narcissistic manipulation to confuse the victim. There is no limit to the cruelty.

The man I married has a sick mind. He also said my deceased friend once made a pass at him. He said, she said to him, "You are cute." In his delusional mind, that translated to her having some attraction to him. The man I married is so unstable. I live here in fear. I know he hates me. I know he is vengeful. I pray for protection.

Veronica

SORROW

August 2, 2024

Today is a difficult day. I just returned from my neighbor and friend's memorial service. It was my friend whom the man I married said made a pass at him. The memorial service was held at her home. It was done exactly as she had planned. Family and friends gathered to honor her memory. You could feel the love all around the room.

I returned home, drowning in self-pity and sorrow. The sorrow I felt was for the loss of my friend's life. The pity was for me. I live in a world where no one expresses love for me. The man I married is consistently cold and indifferent toward me. I am struggling just to stay alive because the man I married and our son have no love for me. How can that be! Lord, please release this pain that consumes my body, mind, and soul.

Veronica

WORK RELIEF

August 10, 2024

Today I went to work as a teacher's assistant. The pay is only $90 per day. I plan to work all week. I don't really enjoy getting up at 5:30 and arriving at work by seven.

However, I will continue to work occasionally just to get away from this house of torture. The man I married continues to treat me as if I am of no significance at all. The pain he inflicts is unrelenting; never-ending. This is a painful way to live. His disorder makes him a hateful and vengeful man. I know it is his illness that makes him behave the way he does. However, I believe he chooses to be cruel to me because he shows kindness to others.

It is by the merciful and powerful forces in the Universe that I am okay; that I have survived this ordeal for over five decades. I am grateful and thankful for the angels who watch over me.

Lord, please help me to maintain a healthy mind and body. Please continue to protect me from the forces that seek to destroy me.

Veronica

NO HAPPINESS HERE

August 11, 2024

The realization that I have been used and abused for decades has me traumatized. There is no joy and no happiness in my life. I cannot recall a time of happiness.

I have lived in misery for many years. It is so difficult to accept the cruelty of the man I married. His hatred runs deeply. He is heartless. He disrespected and betrayed me for so long. I reflect on the years we lived on Hilton Head Island. It was there that I suffered such unrelenting pain. There was physical and mental anguish that nearly killed me. All that time, he happily paraded along, betraying me, deceiving me, laughing at me, and telling people lies about me.

People, some of whom I considered to be friends, believed the charming man I married. They never considered my true character; it was easier to see the picture of me, the man I married, painted for them.

My heart aches, my soul aches, my spirit aches, my body aches, and my mind aches. I do not understand the world I now live in. I am lost; I am broken; I am wounded beyond repair. There is no hope for me. I breathe, but I do not feel alive.

Veronica

INVISIBLE

August 16, 2024

I sit here and listen as my son and his father engage in a happy phone conversation. There is no recognition of me. They laugh and they talk. I sit here as if I am a nonperson. What kind of humans treat other humans in such abusive ways? Lord, please give me the strength to survive this ongoing abuse that I am constantly subjected to by the man I married and our son.

How do you heal from decades of ongoing narcissistic abuse. I am so weary. I live in a traumatized state with a man who hates me. How can someone whom I have lived with for decades hate me? I have not done any harm to this man. I have been a loving and faithful wife all these years. He has abused me, yet I carry no hate in my heart for him.

It has been only recently that I acknowledged the fact that the man I married has always hated me. I reflect and see it so clearly. He disrespected and betrayed me for decades. For many years, he masterfully portrayed himself to me and to the public that he was a loving, devoted husband and father. I now see him for who he really is. I am the only person who knows how unstable he truly is. I do not feel safe living here with him. He deceives others so easily.

Everybody thinks he is a charming, nice guy because that is the believable character role he plays in public. They have not heard nor seen the venom that deluges from him when he becomes enraged. It is a nightmarish experience. It is an unforgettable event that I have witnessed several times. Life with him is almost unbearable. I pray for help and release from this agony.

I breathe, but I do not feel alive.

Veronica

THE DREAM

September 3, 2024

The man I married and I are on a trip to Connecticut to visit family. I had a very strange dream the first night here. The man I married and I were lying in bed in his mother and father's old bedroom. The man I married and I have not slept in the same bed in nearly a year. I made it quite clear that first night that he would remain on his side of the bed and I would remain on mine. That worked out just fine. There was enough space between us that I forgot he was there. At some point, I was jolted awake from a vivid dream. In the dream, the man I married confessed to HHI affair (He has always adamantly denied the affair).

In the dream, he said he loved the woman, and she loved him. He said I stood in the way of their happiness. He needed to discredit me so that he could justify being with her. I woke up suddenly at 5 am.

Wow! Was the Universe speaking to me? Was that part of the healing process? Whatever it was, it was a powerful awakening. I hope I get some relief from this unrelenting pain that consumes my body, my mind, and my soul. I had a dear friend, Folly King, who led a group on dream interpretations when we lived on Hilton Head Island. It was a wonderful experience. I wonder how my deceased friend would have interpreted the dream I had about the man I married.

Veronica

The man I married read my "The Dream" journal writing. His reaction signifies triangulation and projection. He sent me the following message:

From:xxxxxxxxxx

Date: October 10, 2024, at 8:08:11 PM EDT

To: xxxxxxxxxxx

Veronica,

I am going to send this to all the Qigong Leaders. They will see how your mind is maladjusted. I believe you are possessed.

It really affected me when I read, "I believe you are possessed." I felt uneasy. The statement frightened me. What does that mean? Was the man I married deflecting? Does he deem himself to be possessed? Is he trying to pass it on to me? I live in a state of insecurity and terror. I do not know this stranger who resides in this house with me.

"I DESPISE YOU!"

September 6, 2025

I had a wonderful stay in Connecticut. I am happy I was able to make the trip. It had its painful moments. We rode past all three of our former homes. The heartbreaking memories were overwhelming; I cried many tears as we drove past each house. The man I married spoke no words, he showed no emotions.

Last night, I again made the mistake of expressing my feelings about past painful events in this marriage. The man I married became enraged. He said I am always "digging, digging." He used hand gestures of someone digging.

Then he shouted at me, "That is why I despise you!" That statement resonated to my soul. My anxiety level heightened. I wanted to flee the house, but it was night and far too dangerous to leave. There is no way this kind of reaction is normal. Who is this person?

It is now the morning of our departure back to Georgia. He is punishing me with the silent treatment and ignoring me as if I do not exist. After playing the role of a kind and caring person for a short period, the cycle phases of devalue and discard emerge again; it always does.

The man I married is unhinged; I witness his strange reactions and hear his distorted versions of events.. No one else seems to notice the oddities. He manages to behave in seemingly normal ways in the presence of others. I live in fear and uncertainty every day.

I pray for protection. I fear he will try to destroy me in any way possible because his delusional mind tells him I am the enemy. What a frightening world I live in with this man. He continues to portray the image to family and friends that he is a devoted husband. It is all so fake. He wears his mask of deception so well.

I breathe, but I do not feel alive.

Veronica

TRIP TO HILTON HEAD ISLAND

September 17, 2024

We are here, on Hilton Head Island. I fought back the tears as we crossed the bridge to the island. The years we lived here were some of the most painful and terrifying in my life. It was on Hilton Head Island where the emotional and mental abuse were most calculated and most brutal. Painful thoughts and memories are flooding my mind. I am plunged into a deeper state of depression. Lord, please help me to remain strong in mind and body.

"I breathe, but I do not feel alive."

Veronica

RETURN TRIP FROM HILTON HEAD ISLAND

September 19, 2024

The man I married and I returned home safely to Georgia from a trip to Hilton Head Island. During the four-hour ride back to Georgia, not a word was spoken between us. We spoke casually as we unpacked the car. I cooked, and he went to retrieve our dog, Sugar, from our son's house.

When he returned, we ate in separate rooms. He did not utter a word to me. He sits and watches TV. I pass through the room; he does not look at me, nor does he utter a word to me. I cannot continue to live like this. I want to leave, but I am trapped here with this heartless man.

God, please show me the route to escape. My body and my mind cannot endure much more. My hair is falling out. My skin looks terrible. I am a mess.

"I breathe, but I do not feel alive."

Veronica

THE CONFESSION

September 20, 2024

I am so restless. I want to flee this life I am living here with this cruel man. It is worse than living alone. There is someone here, but there is no communication. I broke down and told him I cannot live like this. He is so delusional; he does not see the problem. He deflects and says he cannot communicate with me. In essence, I am the problem.

I could not help myself, I brought up issues of the past. He handled it well for a change. He did not shout out in rage. He came very close for the first time to admitting to his affair on Hilton Head Island. He said the woman was as crazy as I am. It was such a typical narcissistic confession.

I am disgusted that he would make any comparison between me and another woman. This man has no respect for me. I desperately want to flee. God, please help me find a way.

"I breathe, but I do not feel alive."

Veronica

MAJOR LIFE MISTAKE

September 22, 2025

I just had this amazing feeling that I am finally breaking free from the hold this man has on me. I felt total disgust for the deceitful character that defines him. The feeling evolved when I had a memory of a time when we lived on Hilton Head Island.

Our oldest grandson was living with us. I discovered $3,000 I had saved for emergencies had gone missing. Our grandson was the prime suspect. I was angry and disappointed that he stole from me. I initiated the silent treatment against him for a period of time. It was a tactic I learned from the man I married and from my grandmother many years ago. It was a tactic they used often to hurt me. When you live with a narcissist for so long, you can acquire narcissistic traits. I pleaded with our grandson for the truth. He admitted taking some of the money, but declared he did not take all of it. I believe my grandson. I have no proof, but I believe the man I married took the bulk of that money. He allowed our grandson to take the blame.

What kind of man does that? When I confronted the man I married, his response was narcissistic. He said, "How can I steal my own money?" In his delusional mind, he felt justified to take the money I saved for "us." The money was saved for "us," so that equates to it being "his" money. Sick!

Who is this person I have allowed in my life all these decades? How was he able to deceive me for so long? I was too blind to see what was happening right before my eyes all those years. I think I am getting closer and closer to acceptance of who he truly is. He is not a nice person due to the disorder he has. He obviously cannot control his impulses to lie, cheat, and steal.

I must take responsibility for my part in what happened to me. I failed in many ways. I wanted to be with this man so badly. I feel disgust toward myself for wanting him so much. My desire to be with him was a major life mistake.

Veronica

WARRIOR

October 9, 2025

Yesterday was an extremely emotional day for me. I am trying to sort through things in the garage. I found a new watch, five small cameras, and three small telescopes. This was all new stuff in boxes that had never been opened.

I know I should have kept my mouth closed, but the callous waste of money struck a sensitive nerve, causing a reaction. Narcissists do not react well to being questioned. I asked the man I married what was the purpose of buying all that stuff. That did not go well. He became enraged. He picked up a small object and threw it at me. He then rushed out the back door of the garage. I went to the back door and shouted at him to stay away from me. He picked up something from the ground and hurled it in my direction. Then he threw up his arms in what appeared to be utter frustration.

My offense: I asked why he spent money so foolishly. His reaction was abusive and dangerous. I did not feel safe at my home. I was extremely anxious and frightened. My entire body was shaking. I grabbed my purse and car keys; I fled the house and drove away. I was afraid.

This man is becoming unhinged. He is a dangerous stranger. I do not know this man I have lived with for nearly 53 years. I am afraid of him. I accept my role in the situation. I know my actions set him off. I am human with flaws.

I was so distraught and nervous while driving. I nearly had an accident. I went to a Walmart parking lot to be safe. It was not safe for me to drive in that state of mind.

I had concerns for the welfare of the man I married. He had once vaguely alluded to ending his life.. In desperation, I called our son (I never call him; I chose no contact with him for my well-being). I told our son he needed to check on his father. I told him what happened and shared my concerns for his father.

I was hoping for a different outcome, but my son's response to me clearly defined why I must maintain my policy of no contact with him. He did not express concern for his father. His focus was on his perceptions of my instabilities. He started blame shifting; everything is my fault in every situation he brought to the surface. He continued with the implication that I have signs of dementia. He said that other people are coming to the same conclusion about me.

Wow, my anxiety level skyrocketed. He was clearly gaslighting, projecting, deflecting to me. I recognize the manipulative tactics. My thoughts were, "This is hopeless, I am in trouble and possibly in danger." The man I married and our son can no longer control me. They are applying their manipulative tactics to destroy me and to convince others that I am unstable. I am fearful of the man I married, and I am afraid of our son.

I called the National Hotline for Domestic Violence. They listened to me and referred me to a Georgia domestic violence hotline. I called the Georgia hotline and was connected to someone who listened and empathized with my plight. It helped to have someone to listen to me and to not judge me.

I stayed in the parking lot until my nerves were calm. When I returned, the man I married was calm and collected as if nothing had happened. We discussed getting a divorce. He said it is what we need to do because we cannot get along.

I know we need to separate. I know it is the way I am going to survive. Yet, I fear living without him because I do not know another way to live. He is all I have. I know he does not love me and does not care about my well-being. I know he is only concerned about the finances we share.

Our 53 years of marriage mean nothing to him. In his mind, I have always been easily disposable and easily replaceable. That has been my life history with this man. The acknowledgment of that truth devastates and destroys me. I feel disgusted with myself for being too afraid to let him go. I know it is the trauma bond. It is imperative to break the bond; it is not an easy task.. It is like an addiction. I know he is not good for me. Yet, I stay here and endure the abusive behaviors, the lies, the cruelty, and the hatred. That makes respect for myself appear nil. I feel ashamed.

The pain of it all is unbearable. I have irrational thoughts of suicide. No one cares about me. There is no reason for me to be here. There is no hope for the future; I am too old.

My rational mind knows if I kill myself, the man I married and our win. I am the warrior that my maternal grandmother's influences taught me to be. I stay alive another day to fight the forces that try to destroy me.

"I breathe, but I do not feel alive."

Lord, please protect me.

Veronica

SUICIDE NOTES

October 18, 2024

The man I married and I arrived safely back home to Georgia after a five-day stay on Hilton Head Island. I kept my mouth closed so there were no outbursts of engagement as soon as I got back to the home. I was overwhelmed with weakness and despair. I went grocery shopping and then cooked dinner for us.

I was overcome with feelings of despair. I called on God for some relief. I reached for an old family bible I found while going through stuff in the garage.

It was a Bible that the man I married's mother gave to us many years ago. I opened the Bible. There was a shocking surprise.

I found two sealed envelopes that contained suicide notes I had written. One was written to my son, the other to the man I married. The notes were dated January 23, 1993. It was a devastating moment. It confirmed that I have been enduring this abuse for decades. The tears flowed like the waters at Niagara Falls.

I had no idea what was happening to me in 1993. I did not realize I was being brutally abused. I know I was unhappy and depressed. I was having physical and mental ailments. I was having severe dizzy spells quite often. I had to be taken to the emergency room on two occasions. I was taken from home by EMS once. The other time I was taken from the school where I worked in Atlanta. There was nothing physically found to be wrong. A doctor told me I was having panic attacks. I began seeing a psychiatrist. I was prescribed anxiety and depression medications that I took for the next three decades of my life.

I look at this man I married, is so hard to comprehend how I stayed with him and survived all these decades. I allowed him to abuse, use, and disrespect me for so long. He did it for 53 years and continues to be cruel and abusive. There was never any "normal" in this marriage. There was only devastation and destruction. Here I am, still tolerating the abuse because I have no way to escape. This man has never cared about me. That is a hard pill to swallow. I look at him and I wonder what kind of man is he. This cannot be normal.

I am alone; I wish there was just one authentic and genuine person I could trust to share my final time on Earth with. My only child cast me aside as if I were disposable trash. How can a child show no expression of love or empathy for his biological mother who nurtured and raised him? That is not normal! My son exhibits strong narcissistic behaviors.

I have a dear friend who lives onHilton Head Island. She has her own issues, but she listens tome and offers support. She calls me every day. I am blessed and grateful for her presence in my life.

I am grief-stricken, heartbroken, confused, and disillusioned. How could this man deceive, betray, and abuse me for decades? He does not have an ounce of remorse.

His thought is, "You deserve what you get," that is his justification for some of his behaviors. That is not normal.

"I breathe, but I do not feel alive.

Veronica

January 23, 1993

Dear Gumal,

I love you. Remember to be the best you can be. Tell my grandchildren I love them, too.

Love forever,
Mom

My son was 21. There were no grandchildren in 1993.

January 23, 1993

Dear Colon,

I love you. The years with you have been the best in my life.

Please remember: <u>Don't</u>

1. Show my body.
2. Drink too much
3. Forget me.
4. Put me on life support

<u>Do</u>

1. Marry again
2. Have a good life
3. Donate my organs, if you can.

Love forever,
Patsy

I weep for the version of me who wrote this. At that time, she had no clue as to whom and as to what was devastating and destroying her life under the pretense of love.

DEPRESSION

October 20, 2025

This Sunday morning, I awoke with overwhelming feelings of depression. I got up and cooked breakfast for the man I married and me. I then returned to my bed. Finding those suicide notes affected me deeply. It was confirmation that I have been fighting for survival for decades.

I was never living; I was merely surviving. I have tolerated the abusive behaviors of this man for decades, never fully understanding exactly what he was doing to me. I think he believes he is justified for all the deceit, the betrayals, and the manipulations.

None of it was wrong in his view. He was entitled to do whatever he wanted or desired to do. It did not matter who was hurt by his actions. Narcissists are lacking in conscience and remorse.

I am devastated beyond repair.

"I breathe, but I do not feel alive."

Veronica

THE ENCOUNTER

October 26, 2024

I attended my grandson's senior recognition football game with all the family members tonight. I was thrilled to see and hug all the grandchildren. I was happy to see my former daughter-in-law and her parents. I was not happy to see my son's current wife. She did not acknowledge me, and I did not acknowledge her. She and I are not on speaking terms. She has shown me some subtle signs of distrust. My instincts dictate toxicity in her presence. I choose to have no contact with her. I have learned to trust my instincts about some people. I had not spoken to my son in a long time. I knew he had been plotting with his father to get a court order to have me evaluated for some mental disorder. He approached me with a big grin on his face and a gesture to hug me. My instinct dictated to me that he was not being sincere. I turned away and declined his hug.

I know I should have kept my mouth shut, but I didn't. I just wanted my son to realize that I know about his pursuit to get a court order to have me evaluated for some mental disorder.

As we were leaving the game, I said to him, "Please get that court order you want." One of my grandsons heard what I said. My son's response, "I don't know what you are talking about".I laughed and said, "Right," as I kept walking.

When I arrived home, my son called. I missed his call, but somehow pocket called him. He called his father to let him know I was connected to his phone. My son and I began an engaging conversation that confirmed his narcissistic traits. He started with a blatant lie. He said I told his sons they should read the book I wrote that is a total untruth. I never mentioned to my grandchildren that I wrote a book. He gaslighted about past events. He called me a narcissist. He tried to triangulate me with other family members. He implied that people are noticing that I am unstable. He said I have serious mental issues.

I jokingly agreed with all that my son said. I assured him that he is correct in his assessment of me. He was baiting me, but I was not biting. I remained calm. He was agitated by my response. I did not react the way I was supposed to as outlined in a narcissist's script.

My son emphasized that I need help because I am not the same person I used to be. That is so hilarious. I used to be a person who was easily manipulated and controlled. Since he and his father can no longer manipulate and control mark me as being unstable and I need mental care. Wow, this is so mucked up!

I was amazed by how my son so eloquently followed a narcissistic script. His behavior and tactics were all so typical narcissistic. There is no room for doubt; he has strong narcissistic traits. My baby boy is narcissistic just like his father.

I encouraged my son to get the court order. His father has refused to assist him. Two witnesses are required to file.

He asked me to encourage his father to follow through with the pursuit to get a court order for me. I mentioned it to the man I married as my son and I were talking. His father's voice changed to a tone of irritation. He claims the court pursuit is all our son's idea. He refuses to follow through with our plot. That is what he says to my face.

''''''''

I do not feel safe. I do not know what extremes the man I married and our son might take to totally annihilate me. They view me as an enemy and as a threat to them. I live in fear every day.

Lord, please continue to protect me from my son and the man I married. They both have some serious issues; they do not behave like the norm. I believe they are narcissists. They have no care for my well-being. It is as if I am a thorn in their side that needs to be removed.

Veronica.

DEVALUED

November 4, 2024

 I have not written in a while. I am putting forth the effort to get out of this self-pity mode where I have lingered for the past two years; far too long. I have been praying daily for relief from this unrelenting pain that consumes me.

I was getting closer to acceptance that life with the man I married will never change. Then I had an encounter with my son. The pain soars to a higher level. My son, my only child, tries to diminish his mother with harsh words and cruel actions.

My only child told me I am not welcome at his home. His father heard him say that to me during a phone conversation. His father did not flinch; he did not utter a word in my defense. There is something radically wrong here. This behavior cannot be normalized. Their behavior toward me indicates that they despise me, hate me, and loathe me. I am a human being; I do no harm to them.

There is no justification for their abusive treatment of me. There is something drastically wrong with this picture. I live with fear of the two men who were supposed to love and care for me.

I know the man I married over time meticulously orchestrated this situation. He sits back, acts innocently, and watches the scenes play out in the script he has written. I think he is a dangerous person. I am afraid of both of them. I am more fearful of my son than his father.

His father has a vested interest in keeping me around. I have access to money that he cannot touch. I live in this house, buy groceries, cook, clean, and bring in extra money from my job as a substitute teacher. He considers me to be his obedient, loyal, and devoted slave. It is beneficial to keep me around for now. If there were better options for him, I would be disposed of in a heartbeat.

My son, on the other hand, is seeking vengeance. I caused major injury to his ego over a year ago. I demanded he leave my house. I threatened to call the police due to his disrespect and verbal abuse of me inside my home. I am now enemy number one. I have to be punished. It cannot be normal for a mother to feel fearful of her child. I do not want any contact with my precious baby boy, who is now 53 years old. It is a mother's heartbreak. I love my child, but I will no longer tolerate nor accept his disrespect and abuse.

Family and friends would never believe the truth about these two men. They both portray themselves as charming, loving, and benevolent to the outside world. The outside world never sees what happens behind closed doors. They play their masked roles impeccably well for all to see. I see the malevolent side; the frightening personas that lurk behind the masks. I know their truth, and that jeopardizes my existence. I truly believe a higher power has been protecting me all this time and continues to protect me. I am so grateful.

I breathe; I want to feel alive.

Veronica

MARRIAGE COUNSELING

November 19, 2024

Lord, it is another sleepless night for me. My mind will not stop with the racing thoughts. The man I married and I went to a marriage counseling session today. I learned from mistakes of the past of past sessions. My aim was to not say anything that he would perceive as an attack on him. The spoken truth. Is perceived as an attack. Therefore, it was a delicate maneuver with every wordI spoke.

His interaction was so predictable. He was quick to cast blame on me. I listened and remained calm as he lied so easily. My nervous system was predictably affected. I was feeling nervous and anxious. I wanted to flee. However, I remained calm; I did not lose control. I was hoping the therapist would recognize his irrational responses and realize something was awry. Her assessment was that the man I married and I do not like each other. It pained my heart to hear her speak her truth. She had no clue as what to was really happening.

My heart sank; therapists can make situations of narcissistic abuse worse for victims. They too often believe the abusers and cast doubt on the victims. Their wrong assessments can put victims in potential danger.

I know marriage counseling sessions in narcissistic relationships are fruitless. There is no hope for this relationship.. The man I married emotionally discarded me a long time ago. There is no possible come back from the discard. He physically remains in this relationship because of the personal benefits that come with it. That is the painful truth.

The marriage was never about his love for me as a human being, it was only about the benefits he attained from being with me. That is a truth that rips at my heart and my soul. I will never recover from the pain inflicted on me for over five decades.

I do not want to spend my final time on Earth living in this toxic and unhealthy situation. I am trapped. I do not see a path out. Lord, please show me a way to escape before I die.

Veronica

COLD GARAGE

December 7, 2024

Today is a cold December 7, 2024. I met the man I married on a cold December night in 1969. I was 22 years old. My life was forever changed that night 55 years ago. I sit here in a cold garage wrapped in a warm blanket. The garage is my safe place, 55 years later. I am organizing stuff to have a garage sale. I want to sell this house in Georgia and move back to our house on HHI. I pray every day that I can return to that island and let it be the place I spend whatever time I have left on Earth. There is no peace for me in Georgia. There are too many forces working against me.

I am afraid of my son. He tries to gaslight and confuse me when he talks to me. I am blessed to be cognizant of his manipulative tactics. He has been trying to get his father to support him in his attempt to get a court order to have me evaluated. My son and his father are off balance because I am no longer the puppet they can control and manipulate.

I was hoping the move back to Georgia from Hilton Head Island be a better life; it did not happen. It has been a never nightmare. My son and his father have tormented me with nasty and subtle tactics. They so charmingly conceal their abusive behaviors from the eyes of the public.

They easily convince easily convince others that I am the unstable person. It seems there is no acknowledgment of truth anymore. The man I married sits in the warm house seemly content and watches TV.

As usual, there is no conversation and no engagement with me. This is our everyday existence. It is a painful existence. I am fortunate that the Rockdale County High School Special Education department values me as a person. They asked me to substitute for a teacher for the entire month of December.

It is a safe haven for me during the weekdays. I am blessed and honored. I know a higher power watches over me and protects me from the evil that surrounds me. I have conducted extensive research. I now have a better understanding of what happened to me throughout the decades of being with this man. It does not paint a pretty picture. I am so lucky to have survived. I truly believe I have been protected and spared by God or some force in the Universe.

The man I married and our son have tried to destroy me with their lies and manipulative tactics. I have been broken so many times. There were times when I wanted to give up, but the warrior in me stood strong to continue to fight this never-ending psychological war.

I have been having nightmares about the years we lived on Hilton Head Island. It was the worst time in this marriage. My nightmares carry the message that during the years on Hilton Head Island, the man I married wanted me gone so that he could be with another woman. I truly believed he hoped I would die or that I would commit suicide. I can remember wanting to die. He was meticulously tormenting me. His behavior was cruel and evil. He labeled me a bitch; he rejected me; he isolated me. He was someone who morphed from the person I loved and adored to become a horrible stranger.

I was mentally and physically ill. I was taking three different types of prescribed antidepressant pills daily. I was taking anxiety pills nightly to sleep. I am fortunate to have survived because I drank alcohol at night and ingested anxiety pills. It was what I needed to do in order to sleep. I was stressed and restless; I could not sleep. The man I married expressed no concern for me. He witnessed my struggles for survival. I believe he wanted me to disappear from this Earth.

All the time, the man I married appeared content and happy. He was feeding friends, family, and others lies about me. They believed him.

He was setting me up. If something happened to me, everyone would have rallied around him with sympathy. That would have brought him great joy. However, his plan for my demise did not come to fruition because a higher power was protecting me.

I hope that one day, more people will become aware of narcissism and the devastation and destruction it inflicts on innocent people.

Veronica

ACCEPTANCE

December 22, 2024

Today is Sunday, December 22, 2024. The man I married and I are traveling to Hilton Head Island for Christmas. We have been riding for about two hours now. Not one word has been spoken by either of us.

This is no way to live life. The man I married could easily drive away and leave me stranded anywhere. He did that many times when we were younger. I am prepared with my phone and with money at all times.

I am trapped in a loveless marriage. When I married this man on December 27, 1971, I thought I married the man of my dreams. It is now 53 years later, and I realize I am married to the man of my nightmares. I feel empathy for this man. He will be stuck in a fantasy world forever. I was stuck in that world with him for 53 years. I can forgive him for all he has done to me, except for one thing: taking my son from me. He is responsible for the estrangement between my son and me. This is unforgivable.

Beginning our 54th year together, I finally feel liberated; liberated from the control, manipulations, betrayals, cheating, and lying. I am free because I do not care anymore. Acceptance is the key that opens the door to freedom. I finally accept the fact that the man I married never had any love for me. He has a personality disorder that makes him incapable of loving anyone. People like him are self-centered; they only care about themselves. When they say, "I love you," they really mean, "I use you." They use and abuse people throughout their lives.

There is no hope for a better life for me; my life is done. "I breathe, but I do not feel alive." I write because I want people to be aware that people like the man I married exist in society. People need to be protected from toxic, abusive people. They are dangerous and destructive. They suck the life out of people. Many victims suffering mental, emotional, and psychological abuse do not survive.

The pain becomes too much. They choose death over a life of unrelenting pain. I had a friend whose husband was boldly cheating and disrespecting her publicly. Her life ended under a bridge in a river. Why did her life end alone in the murky waters of a river?

A narcissist could easily relish the sympathy displayed to him/her after the death of a spouse. The narcissist could devour the attention as if it were a fine meal. The narcissist could play an Academy Award-winning role as the grieving spouse.

I will not unalive myself. I honestly believe that has been an ongoing dream for the man I married over the years. But that is not God's plan for me. The truth needs to be spoken. My silence will come the day I die.

Veronica

SILENT TREATMENT

December 25, 2024

Lord, no human being should have to live like this. The man I married and I are in a hotel on Hilton Head Island. We sit in this room hour after hour, and not one word is spoken between us. It is psychological and emotional abuse. He does it purposely. He wants me to break down and beg him for attention. In that way, he thinks he can regain control and power over me. The silent treatment is a cruel tactic used by the narcissist.

I needed a safe space away from the toxicity that exists in the room. I am currently down in the lobby writing this. I feel a sense of relief. My mind and my body will not be able to hold up to this abuse much longer. I wish I could flee and never look back.

The man I married is in for a rude awakening; I am so done with him. The trauma bond has been broken. I do not give a fuck what he does or with whom he does it. Yes, I fear him. He is an unstable and deceitful person. In his delusional world, I am the enemy. He will do anything to hurt me, as hurting me fuels him and makes him feel better. It has always been like that in our relationship. I was always confused by his behavior, trying so hard to please him and to make him happy, but it was all in vain. I did not have the knowledge I now have.

It is so scary because no one knows how sick and unstable this man is. I am the only person who knows the truth. No one would believe me.

They do not see or experience the abuse. He never shows the public the dark side that lurks behind the mask of deception. His public image is sacred. He wants everyone to believe he is kind, charming, and honest. That is the person the public knows, loves, and respects. I honor his family and the friends who have this positive image of the man I married. That is the person they know. I understand and I respect their perception of the man I married. That is not the man I know. In his delusional mind, that makes me the enemy. He will strive to make me an unstable being in the eyes of the public. They will remain blind to the truth. It is not okay, but I must accept what is.

Veronica

OUR ANNIVERSARY

December 27, 2024

Today, December 27, 2024, marks the 53rd anniversary of my wedding day. It is a day I wish never happened. In a normal relationship, a husband and wife would happily celebrate as a blessed milestone in their lives. There was no mention of our anniversary. On any given day, the man I married only says what is absolutely necessary to say to me.

So, today is no different. The pain in my being is excruciating. That is abuse. It takes a toll on my mind, body, and soul. He does not care how much he hurts me. My feelings are of no significance to him. I am of no significance to him. This is the painful truth. It devastates me; it destroys me. I struggle to survive. The sad part is that he does not possess the capacity to care. It is due to the personality disorder I truly believe he has. Nothing can change that. There were never any real happy celebrations of our decades together. There might have been an occasional card a few times. There were no special gifts at Christmas nor for birthdays. I was okay with it; I was just so happy to be with him. Being with him, I used to think, was the greatest gift I could have received.

I know that he has a personality disorder that prevents him from behaving like what I view the norm. He does not have the same emotions that most people have. He is only concerned about what benefits him. He cannot change; it is who he is. He has no conscience and no remorse when it comes to how he treats me. He feels entitlement; he believes he is special; and he believes he is better than me.

We are riding back home to Georgia as I write. It is 9:45. We left at 7:00. Not a word has been spoken in this car. People cannot imagine my feelings of torment and anguish.

There was a bright side to our stay on the island. We had a wonderful visit with my friend. She treated us to a nice Christmas dinner with her senior friends. We have been friends for a very long time. She calls me every night at 6 pm. She has supported and believed in me throughout this two-year journey with the unmasked version of the man I married. I am so thankful and blessed to have her in my life.

My friend will be 85 next month. Her health is deteriorating. I hope she and I survive until my planned return to live on Hilton Head Island in July.

I am thankful for the smallest blessings.

Veronica

DEATH CALENDAR DATE

January 22, 2025

I have not expressed my feelings in a while. I have been feeling positive because I work every day at Rockdale County High School. It is my safe place to be during the day. Monday was a holiday, Tuesday and Wednesday were snow days. I have been stuck in misery at home with the man I married.

Lately, there has been a dramatic change in his behavior. He has been talking to me as if I really exist. He is so fucking fake and deceitful. I understand fully what he is doing.

It is so obviously textbook narcissistic behavior if you have studied the behaviors of narcissists. The man I married knows he has lost control of me. He is trying every tactic in his bag of manipulative tricks. Stonewalling and silent treatments did not work. I did not come begging to him for a crumb of attention or acknowledgement like I had been trained to do for decades. That degrading behavior has long expired; I know my worth.

I have been isolated from my primary family. I do not get to see our grandchildren. Our son has banned me from his house. I sit back at home alone as the man I married is welcomed to our son's home to enjoy family time with them. It hurts me deeply, but I remain silent. I have learned not to share my pain; it only feeds his ego.

I know he has vengeance in his heart against me. I live in constant fear of what his plans are to hurt or harm me mentally, physically, or financially. I do not trust anything he does or says. This is a very difficult life I am living.

Today, I watched a video as the funeral director covered my sister-in-law's face and closed her coffin. It was a profound and sad moment; a life had ended; a person never to be seen again. I wonder what that will be like? Death is the final release from all physical and mental pain. There is a death date written on a calendar for every living being. Like many others, I wonder what my calendar death date is. That will be my day of peace.

Veronica

MY INSTINCTS

February 5, 2025

Today is Wednesday, Feb 5, 2025. I am about to go to bed. My instincts are warning me that I am not safe in my home. The man I married has not engaged in conversations with me in over two years.

Now, suddenly, he talks to me as if he recognizes me as a human being. He recently started getting up early with me when I am preparing to go to work at Rockdale County High School. I cook breakfast for both of us. We eat at the table together.

On cold days, he warms the car for me. This sudden change in his behavior is quite alarming to me. I have listened to narcissism experts on YouTube. They describe this type of behavior as a possible calm before the storm. Their theory is that the narcissist fakes a change to throw the victim off balance. However, at the same time, the narcissist is possibly plotting revenge against the victim. This change is frightening to me. I do not know what to expect from this man.

Every day I live in fear that a storm might come. I cannot erase the memory of the times when this man looked me in my face and said he hated me; said he despised me. I truly believe he has evil and destructive thoughts in his head in regards to me.

I pray for protection.

Veronica

VALENTINE'S DAY

February 14, 2025

Today is February 14th, 2025, Valentine's Day. The man I married was up early. Silly me, I kept hoping he would say, "Happy Valentine's Day."

He did not utter a word in that regard. It is what I expected, but it hurts so much to be devalued, unloved, and unappreciated. I worked at Rockdale County High School today. Two 10th graders drew pictures and gave them to me. Their gesture of love and kindness brought tears to my eyes. I asked them if I looked sad; both nodded in the affirmative. I fought back my tears. It was a very emotional moment.

I wondered all day at work if the man I married would unexpectedly get me something for Valentine's Day. When I arrived home, there was a dollar store gift bag on the counter. It was a bag he had been about to throw into the trash the previous week. I had told him to save it because I might need it one day.

Last week, he wanted chocolate candy. I found some special packs of chocolate at Aldi and I bought a few of them for him. The small dollar store bag that would have been trashed last week was now stuffed with the same kind of chocolates I had purchased from Aldi's.

Is this your gift to me on Valentine's Day? There was no card. His cruel gesture devastated me. It broke my heart into a thousand pieces again. I was insulted. I just lost it. This man has no respect or any human feelings for me. His response to my outburst on this Valentine's Day was to say I am insane and that I need help. So typical of a narcissist.

I told him I am done. I want a divorce. I can no longer live like this. He continues to do and say hurtful and harmful things. He tries to invalidate me at every level. My body cannot take much more. I believe I am going to die soon if I continue to stay with this man.

My nervous system became off balance, sending me into flight/fight survival mode. I fled the house. I am parked at a Walmart parking lot. I do not want to return to that house of torment, but I do not have any place to go. So, I sit here, lost in this vast world all alone.

I am afraid of the man I married. I know he wants to destroy me. No one knows how dangerous he is. No one believes or knows the danger I am in. They would never believe that this charming man would abuse his wife. He will tell lies about me, and people will believe him. This is a nightmare. I pray for protection.

I pray that I will be shown a safe path to freedom.

Veronica

NOT WORTHY

February 15, 2025

I had the energy to work in the garage this morning. I am struggling to stay strong. Yesterday was such a painful day. The man I married proved to me how unworthy he thinks I am. It is excruciatingly painful to know that I am not worthy of a $10 box of candy and a card on Valentine's Day. The pain of that is insurmountable. He is cruel and cold-hearted toward me. Yet, he so convincingly shows love and kindness to others. This is total madness. The devastation and destruction that are imposed on victims by people like the man I married are indescribable.

Now that I have said I want a divorce, I know the abuse is going to intensify. He can be vengeful. He will lie and convince people that I am the problem. Most will believe him. They will never question the validity of what he is saying about me.

I fear our son will stand up for his father against me. Our son will align with his father just to destroy me. It is a mother's heartbreak beyond repair. I want and I need to escape from this abuse I have endured for decades.

Lord, please lead me toward a place of peace. I am so weary.

Veronica

DANGER

February 17, 2025

My body is telling me I am in danger. It is 5:30 AM. I just got up and went to the bathroom. When I came out of the bathroom, the man I married was standing in the dark just about 6 feet from the bathroom. I screamed out in fear because I was shocked to see him there. He said he was concerned because I was up, and he could not sleep. I was shaking like a leaf on a tree. I went back into my bedroom and closed the door. It is not unusual for me to be up that early. I get up every morning at 5:30 to prepare for work at Rockdale County High School. I am home for the week because schools are closed for winter break.

I told the man I married a few days ago that I want a divorce. Experts say the most dangerous time in an abusive relationship is when the victim decides to leave.

I do not feel safe.

Veronica

HEAVY BURDEN

May 1, 2025

The past two years have been a journey that I never would have imagined I would travel in my lifetime. I am so weary. The burden I carry is too heavy. I pray every day for guidance and protection. I have received many blessings this year. I worked for 5 months at Rockdale County High School. It has been my daily safe haven. I have almost finished a new book I have written on narcissistic abuse. I am grateful.

I write this as I sit in my car at a Walmart parking lot. I worked today at Rockdale County High School. I came here because I do not want to go home to face what awaits me there every day. The man I married is not stable. I fear what his plans are for me. I live with anxiety and fear every day. I know the solution is to walk away, but it is just not that simple. I am old and I need to have some financial security. So, I stay.

There are just two more months before the renters move from our house on HHI. My plan is to move back as soon as they move out. The mortgage is too much for me to pay alone. The man I married plans to move back, also. I need his financial help to pay the mortgage.

We plan to sell this house in Georgia. I have to be so careful. He is so sneaky and deceitful. He is not trustworthy. What he says and what he does can be opposites.

I pray that God will continue to protect me and keep me safe.

Veronica

PREDATOR AND PREY

June 4, 2025

It is getting closer to the time for me to move back to Hilton Head Island. I am overwhelmed by how much I have to do. The house is not ready to be put on the market. I am so depressed; I can hardly function. My long-time friend, Carol, died suddenly. I spoke with her as usual at 6 pm, and then she died during the night. Carol's sudden death set me back. We talked every day for the past two years since I left Hilton Head Island. She was my inspiration to get back to Hilton Head Island. We were both so excited. That excitement is gone and has been replaced with grief.

The man I married is talking to me sometimes like I am human. He probably thinks he is regaining his control over me. That will never happen. I know how the game is played now.

He rarely spoke to me for the past two years. It has been agonizingly painful living in a house with a person who does not acknowledge my existence as a human being. He has suddenly changed and is portraying a different persona. It is like one person moved out and another person has moved in. He has an agenda for this change in behavior; I am not sure what it is. I just know it is not for my benefit.

People see the kindhearted, innocent version that he portrays for an audience of family, friends, and strangers. They do not know the man who lurks behind the mask.

He only reveals himself to me because I am the recipient of all his negativity and toxicity. I am the one he speaks to with a venomous tone of hatred and disgust. His past actions toward me have tormented my soul. I will never recover from the devastation and destruction he has imposed onto my body, mind, and soul.

I do not know if he is truly aware of the damage he has caused. His mind does not function like the norm. I remember long before I educated myself on narcissism, he would often say he had to protect himself. I thought it was a rather odd statement. That is the way he has lived his life, always in a protective mode. His self-protective mode created much pain for others who crossed paths with him.

He did not care about the pain of others. He only cared about himself, and he did whatever to ensure that "self" had all needs, wants, and desires satisfied. That is the way it works in the life of a narcissistic person. He was the predator and I was his prey that he happily controlled, manipulated, betrayed, and deceived for over five decades.

I no longer care for contact with the people who do not believe me or who doubt my sanity. Stay in your lane, and I will stay in mine. You will never understand my journey.

Veronica

KILLING FORCE

June 7, 2025

Today, I sit in the garage. This is my place of peace. There is a TV and a couch. There is a window and an exit door to the backyard. I cooked earlier, even though I was experiencing a lot of pain. The warrior in me will not let me give up. It takes a massive amount of strength to keep moving forward when your body aches.

I was doing fine when I was working. I was walking 10, 000 steps each day. Some days I did several miles on the Nordic track bike. Now, I am suddenly experiencing excruciating pain on my right side. It is the side of my hip replacement that was done 12 years ago. Pain extends from my hip to my ankle. I cannot meet my steps goal anymore. It is too painful to walk.

This is a major setback for me. There is so much to do in this garage. I do not have the energy to do anything.

I know this is due to the trauma that I am living created by decades of narcissist abuse. Narcissistic abuse is a killing force. It attacks your body, mind, and soul. I have been struggling to survive for decades.

I stay out of the man I married's space. I have to be so careful what I say and what I do. If anything happens here, he will easily shift all the blame to me. People will believe him because he is so convincing. He lies so easily, especially when it paints him as the hero or the victim.

He is capable of doing or saying anything that cast doubt and negativity onto me. He will easily tell people tales about me to make me seem unstable or the bad person in this relationship. This life is a never ending nightmare.

No one believes the depth of cruelty and evil that lingers behind the mask of the man I married. I am totally convinced that his mind is out of sync with what is considered the norm. He is impulsive, irrational, and deceitful. These are facts, I know him as well as anyone can know a person like him. Yet, I really do not know him at all , and I have been connected to him for over 54 years. He does not know me; he does not want to know me. To him, I am not human, I am a supply. Supply is a psychological term. I only exist to provide for him and to serve him as if I am a slave.

I am not vengeful. I just want my truth to be known. I am far from perfect. I am flawed like all humans. I have made mistakes. But I never do anything to intentionally hurt another human. I care about what happens to others. I have emotions of sympathy, compassion, and empathy.

There are people who know what my true, authentic character is. However, people in the man I married's circle believe whatever he says about me. They are so wrong. It hurts me so deeply that people will never understand nor accept my truth.

I am grateful to survive and to live another day. I pray for my health to be restored so that I can follow through with my plan to move back to Hilton Head Island by July.

Lord, please continue to guide me and to protect me.

Veronica

RETURNING TO THE SCENE

June 20, 2025

The man I married and I are selling this house in Georgia and moving back to Hilton Head Island. I have lived in this house with him for the past two years, enduring unrelenting pain. During that time, everything changed, and so much was revealed. It was here, in this house, that the mask finally fell. I saw him for who he truly is. He is not the man he pretends to be to family and friends. I witnessed and experienced the cold, detached figure who barely acknowledged me for two full years. I was invisible. I was not viewed or treated as human. The decision to move was mine. Now that we are leaving, he has shifted. He speaks to me, engages with me, and works diligently to pack boxes in preparation for the move. It is as if the two years of rejection never happened.

It is as if the man who crushed me under silence for two long and painful years is now offering a calm voice to settle my nerves. I know it is not real. I have lived this cycle too long to be fooled.

We no longer spend time around friends or family together, so no one witnesses this shift in his demeanor. I worry that during phone calls, friends might overhear him speaking gently in the background. They might assume we are fine. It is just enough to plant doubt about what I have shared, just enough to make them question if I was exaggerating. That is the cruelty of it all. He doesn't need a full audience, just a whisper of kindness at the right moment can erase years of harm in the minds of those who do not understand the depth of narcissistic abuse.

I am not going back with him. I am going back with me, the woman who sees and listens to her own truth.

The woman who no longer waits for others to validate her existence. I know his kindness is a performance. I will no longer be the character in the script he has written for me.

Veronica

STREET VISIT

June 28, 2025

Today was one of my grandsons' 14th birthdays. I am no longer welcome in my son's home, but I decided I would not let that stop me from showing my love. I called my grandson and asked him to meet me outside; I had a gift for him.

The man I married drove me. As we pulled up, two of my grandsons were already waiting on the sidewalk. They came to the car door and greeted me with open arms and warm smiles. They went inside to tell their two brothers, their stepbrother, and their stepsister that I was outside. They all returned to the street and hugged me. It was a happy moment in time; it was a painful moment in time. A moment in time that allowed a grandmother to greet her grandchildren on the street in front of a house that rejects her. I did not see my son nor his wife. I considered that to be a peaceful blessing. I was very nervous about going. I was led by motivation, strength, and courage. I followed the path of a loving grandmother's heart. I stood at the edge of their world, and my grandchildren came to meet me there.

Love found a way to show itself on the street.

Veronica

VISIT TO OUR HOUSE ON HILTON HEAD ISLAND

June 6, 2025

The renters moved out of our house on June 30th. The man I married and I visited our home on Hilton Head Island during the 4th of July week. I had strange feelings being back in my home on Hilton Head Island. My view of the home was different. It felt as if the rooms and the furniture had changed. In reality, nothing in the home had changed.

The reality was that I had changed. I was no longer the heartbroken, drowning in depression, and lost soul who once resided there. I was no longer the love-sick woman waiting for the man I married to return from his adventures socializing with his Qigong group. I was no longer the woman left in isolation while he made his desired connections.

I suffered silently for years in my home on Hilton Head Island. The walls absorbed my tears. The floors knew the weight of my footsteps when I felt too broken to stand up straight. I was slowly withering in a place that should have been safe; my home.

During my first visit back, I saw the house with new eyes. I saw the trees outside; they looked greener. The rooms evoked feelings of hope and possibilities. I carry the pain and the memories of what life was once like in this home.

I want to release the pain and the sad memories of that place in time. I want to reenter with hope and possibilities, a brighter and happier future.

I now understand: *"If it is to be, it is up to me."*

Tomorrow, we will return to Georgia to prepare the other house to sell. I am not just cleaning out, I will be clearing space for a new life. When I return to Hilton Head Island to live, I will not be the woman I once was. I will return as a survivor to see the beauty and the light in a place that was once dark and life-threatening.

THE NIGHT I BEGGED

July 15, 2025

The movers came late today. It was after 8 pm when they left. The man I married was getting ready to drive to Hilton Head Island. Something felt wrong.

He seemed unstable, off-balance, disconnected. I did not feel it was safe. I was worried. I spoke up. I begged him and pleaded with him not to leave at night.

His response? He shouted with rage, *"What is wrong with you?"*

His face twisted in disgust as if my concern for his safety was an insult to his pride. I stood there, devastated. It was not because I needed him or wanted him. It was because I did not want harm to come to him. I did not feel it was safe for him to drive at night. He shouted for me to move away from him and that he was leaving. That was the moment I knew there was nothing left. Fifty-four years living with this man, and he does not treat me with human regard. As he drove away, I collapsed to the floor in gut-wrenching tears. How can this be my reality?

On this day, July 15, 2025, I vow to never beg for anything from anyone ever again in life. The man I married saw my begging as my weakness, and that moment confirmed his superiority to me in his delusional mind. That will never happen again. This relationship is over and done. I have my dignity. I need my freedom from this trap that I live in with this disordered man that no one sees but me.

God, please send angels to help me. I am so weary

Veronica

PSYCHIATRIST SESSIONS

July 17, 2025

Today I felt broken and devastated.

I had a FaceTime session with a psychiatrist who was supposed to assess my mental state. I told him everything about the man I married, about my son, about the years of emotional and psychological torment I have endured. I desperately needed him to see me, to hear my voice, and to recognize the suffering behind my words.

After my session, the man I married had a session. When the psychiatrist came back to me, he said nothing was wrong with the man I married. He concluded that it is time for us to go our separate ways. I asked him, *Do you believe I am an abused wife?*

He did not answer. He just made a small gesture with his hands as if to say, *Who knows?* His hand motion cut deeper than any words. So this is it? A lifetime of being invisible, unheard, unloved, and now even the professionals can not see it? I was devastated.

Then the man I married called. We spoke about the session. He said, "We just don't get along." As if five decades of cruelty, of silence, of punishment and manipulation could be reduced to a disagreement. He said that for now, we have to stay together for financial reasons.

I hate how broken this makes me feel. I hate that part of me still clings to the crumbs. I hate that his call gave me a flicker of relief, that he *talked* to me. What kind of survival is this?

Why do I fear living without this cruel man?

Why does the idea of being alone feel worse than staying trapped?

Is it the years of conditioning? The loneliness? The financial chains? Or is it that I have never truly been allowed to exist *without* him?

Today, I felt so low, so unwanted, so erased. I felt suicidal. I do not want to live like this. There is no hope for me.

Veronica

Triangulation

Triangulation is a manipulative tactic narcissists use to draw a third person into a relationship dynamic. The purpose is not to bring clarity, but to create confusion, competition, and emotional imbalance. It allows the narcissist to control the narrative, boost their ego, and shift blame, all while keeping the victim off balance. The narcissist will position themselves as the hero, the rescuer, or the victim, whichever role serves them best in the moment. The man I married used triangulation often. He would tell me about a female "friend" going through a difficult time. It was someone from work or a social group. He always cast himself as the kind, compassionate helper. And I, lost in my need to believe in him, admired what I thought was his benevolence.

It was not benevolence. It was deception. These women were not just friends. They were likely his romantic partners. By casually inserting them into our conversations, he was planting seeds of confusion while secretly betraying me. I did not see it then. I do now.

That is the nature of triangulation: subtle, cruel, and deliberate. It erodes trust, blurs reality, and leaves you questioning yourself while the narcissist walks away untouched and still looking like the good one.

Covert Triangulation

Covert triangulation is a subtle but devastating form of emotional manipulation, often used by narcissists to divide and conquer relationships. Covert triangulation happens in the shadows. It is silent, disguised, and often undetectable until the damage is already done.

The emotional distance between my son and me did not come from a single event. It crept in slowly, over the years, so quietly that I did not see it happening.

Now I understand it for what it was: **covert triangulation.**

The man I married never had to tell my son to stop loving me. He simply withheld affection from me in my son's presence. In the presence of my son, the man I married told family and friends that my son was the only reason he married me. He showed our son that I was not someone to respect or to value.

My son witnessed me trying to keep the peace in the house. I was the one who was always apologizing, always explaining, always walking on eggshells. I was the *"emotional"* one. I was the *"problem."* Meanwhile, the man I married made sure he was seen as the calm one, the reasonable one, the one who always knew best.

I remember one moment that still lingers. My son and I were sitting in his kitchen. I tried to open up to him.

He looked at me with cold eyes and said, *"You are always trying to be the victim."*

That broke something inside me.

That is what covert triangulation does.

It steals the bond between a mother and child without leaving fingerprints.

Triangulation Trauma

Triangulation trauma is when a victim, often the mother, is emotionally isolated by the two people she loves. One is a narcissistic father/husband. The other is a child who is raised under the father's shadow. The child is shaped by years of manipulation, silence, and emotional conditioning.

Triangulation trauma remained prevalent in my family for a very long time. I was the one who tried to hold the family together. I was easily sacrificed. The man I married emotionally rejected me long ago. The deeper wounds came when our son began echoing his father's cruelty, blame, and detachment. It was slow, almost invisible. It was there in a shift in tone, a side glance, a silence when I needed his voice. It was the quiet joining of two men I loved against me.

They bonded through shared criticisms, shared doubts, and shared conversations I was never part of. Conversations that said I was the problem; I needed to be fixed; I needed to be silenced. I was the wife and the mother who was dismissed.

Often, friends and family will witness it unfold, and they will choose comfort over courage. So the triangle holds firm. One person stands alone at its center surrounded by a wall of denial.

This is what trauma triangulation does:

- It leaves you doubting your reality.

- It makes you question your worth.

- It strips you of safety even in your own home and your own body.

Martha Pike's Traumatizing Diagnosis

In June 2024, I shocked the man I married when I suddenly left home and drove to Hilton Head Island, South Carolina. He did not respond well to my departure.

While I was gone, he contacted someone we had both once known socially, a woman I had not spoken to in years. The man I married must have shared extensive details about me with this woman. She responded by sending him a series of messages, which I could also see, filled with frightening and damaging assumptions about my mental state. When I read them, my nervous system collapsed. My heart pounded, my anxiety skyrocketed, and I became disoriented with fear.

For the record, the woman's real name is Martha Pike. I debated whether to use her real name. But the truth is this, her actions endangered my life. I believe what she did was not only reckless, but unethical and dangerous. This is not a character attack on her. This is a factual account of what she wrote about me without ever speaking to me, seeing me, or hearing my side.

Martha and I were never close, but we once shared loose social connections through a Qi Gong group. She was friendly with the man I married. At the time of these events, we had not spoken in years.

What follows are the text messages she sent. According to her, she is both a nurse and a psychologist. What her qualifications are, I cannot confirm.

What I can confirm is that she diagnosed me from a distance based solely on the words of a man who has psychologically abused me for decades. She never reached out to me. She never asked what I was experiencing. She never saw me. She used real names; I used initials to protect the identity of the people Martha Pike mentioned in her text messages. She wrote:

"CC, stay safe, both you and your son, and even DB too! Unfortunately, Veronica sounds delusional, very paranoid, with the false ideation that you have been having an affair with DB. This can make her a danger to all three of you. Perhaps letting DB know about how mentally ill Veronica is and that she is living with KC right now might spare poor DB any grief from Veronica's paranoid delusional ideation, because she might try to locate DB and try to harm her. She is very mentally ill and unstable right now. For all of you right now. Keep me posted if you want me to talk to DB about all of this. I will intervene for you."

And later:

"Hey, CC, it's Martha... I just laid it flat out about her paranoid and delusional thinking, and she definitely needs help. I told you she needs to be committed. I don't know if you have a doctor... that could force her to be committed because her paranoia scares me. If she had a gun, she could use it. That's my concern... there is a name for this type of ideation... and they just can't pull themselves out of it without medication and psychiatric care.

So I want you to protect yourself... I mean that. Call me anytime... I'll walk you through anything that I would do as a psychologist when I had to have people committed... she is reaching this dangerous level... I care very much about you, and Veronica can get real treatment and help. I think you need to distance yourself from her and tell your son that too... she concerns me, truly..."

When I read those messages, I went into complete shock. The woman I once considered a friend had joined forces knowingly or unknowingly with a man who has gaslighted and manipulated me for decades. Her language mirrored the tactics of narcissistic triangulation: bringing a third party into conflict to discredit and isolate the target.

The man I married weaponized her words against me. Her unsolicited "diagnosis," drawn entirely from his perspective, added fuel to his efforts to portray me as mentally unwell. In truth, I was terrified and exhausted, but not delusional and not dangerous. I was a woman trying to survive.

Out of fear for my safety, I called the National Domestic Violence Hotline. They helped me connect with a women's shelter in Georgia. I drove back from South Carolina to Georgia. I was led by a deputy sheriff escort to the shelter, where I remained for 21 days. I had no other place to go. I was completely alone and afraid.

While I was at the shelter, the man I married reported me missing. I was eventually stopped by the police. When I explained the situation, the policewoman believed me. She immediately called off the missing person alert and gave me her personal number. I will never forget her compassion.

This chapter of my life nearly broke me. I still live with the fear that my own son, influenced by the lies of his father and the "diagnosis" of Martha Pike, a woman who had not seen me in years, will one day succeed in his efforts to have me committed.

I share this not to accuse. I share this because it is my truth. I share because it happened. I share because it matters.

If I See Martha Pike Again

If I see Martha Pike again,
I will not flinch.
I will not fold.
I will not explain myself to the woman who took five minutes of my voice and turned it into a diagnosis.

If I see Martha Pike again,
I will not soften my truth to make her more comfortable.
I will not bow to her spiritual title or her social standing.
Let her carry the calm smile and the clean reputation.
I carry the wounds.

Martha Pike did not need to know me. She just needed to believe the man I married. With that belief, she gave my son permission to question my sanity, to rewrite my motherhood, to discard me.

She became another arm of the abuse cloaked in "concern." If I see Martha Pike again, I will not forget that she called me dangerous. She said I was a threat to my son and to the man I married. She tried to unmake me with words spoken in rooms I was not allowed to enter.

If I see Martha Pike again,

I will not speak.

I do not need to be heard by those who never asked who I was before deciding what I am.

I am not unstable.

I am not dangerous.

I am not defeated.

I am the voice they tried to silence.

I am still here, the lone warrior whom my grandmother molded me to be.

The Smear Campaign

One of the most devastating forms of narcissistic abuse is the smear campaign.

It is when the abuser rewrites your story and shares it with the world before you even get the chance to speak. They distort your truth, question your sanity, and destroy your credibility one quiet lie at a time.

The man I married told others, even our neighbors, that I was suffering from dementia.

He planted seeds of doubt with people who once knew me as strong and intelligent. He told Martha Pike things that led her to question my mental stability. He knew exactly what he was doing. My son, my own child, echoed the same lie. They both created a false narrative designed to silence me, to discredit me, to destroy me. This is not uncommon. Victims of narcissistic abuse are often portrayed as "crazy," "unstable," or "mentally ill." It is a calculated tactic to ensure that when we finally find the courage to speak, no one will listen.

I tried to explain. I tried to defend myself. The more I spoke, the more people believed them. It is because the narcissist tells their version early, often, and with confidence. Planting little seeds that grow into doubt about you for others to see.

If someone engages in a smear campaign against you, please hear me:

Do not chase their lies. Trying to correct every rumor, every whisper, every false accusation will only wear you down.

The sad truth is that most people will believe the abuser. Not because the abuser is more honest, but because they got there first. It is easier to believe a lie than to face the truth about abuse.

You may lose your reputation, your relationships, even your own child to their campaign of destruction. You will not lose your truth. Your dignity will say more than their smear campaign ever could.

Gaslighting

Gaslighting is a deliberate form of psychological manipulation designed to make a person doubt their own memory, perception, and sanity. The abuser denies events that happened, twists words, rewrites history, or flat-out lies. The goal is to have the victim question what is real.

Sometimes, gaslighting is subtle. It could be a raised eyebrow, a dismissive laugh, or a carefully chosen phrase meant to undermine your confidence. Over time, it eats away at your trust in yourself until you feel like you cannot rely on your own thoughts or feelings.

The result is devastating. You start apologizing for things you did not do, doubting events you lived through, and seeking the abuser's version of reality because yours no longer feels certain. This is exactly what the abuser wants. He wants control over not just your actions, but your very mind.

Gaslighting is abuse. It is intentional, it is destructive, and it leaves deep psychological scars. Recognizing it is the first step to breaking free.

If someone constantly makes you question your own reality, understand this: it is not because you are weak or forgetful; it is because they are manipulating you. Your reality matters. Your memory matters. You have the right to trust yourself again.

Invalidation

Invalidation is the act of dismissing, minimizing, or rejecting another person's thoughts, feelings, or experiences. It tells the victim, directly or indirectly, that their emotions are wrong, exaggerated, or unimportant.

In narcissistic abuse, invalidation is a constant undercurrent. It can sound like, "You're too sensitive," "That didn't happen," or "You're overreacting." Over time, these words wear down your confidence in your own emotions and instincts. You begin to silence yourself before you even speak, believing no one will understand or care.

Invalidation is more than hurtful; it is destructive. It strips away a victim's emotional safety, leaving them isolated inside their own pain. The abuser benefits when you stop expressing your feelings, because silence makes control easier.

Recognizing invalidation is a crucial step toward reclaiming your voice. You have the right to your feelings, your truth, and your own emotional reality. If your emotions are constantly dismissed, please know this: your feelings are valid, your experiences matter, and you deserve to be heard. Your truth does not need anyone else's approval to be real.

Abandonment

Abandonment evokes a pain that shatters the heart. It bewilders the mind. It wounds the soul. It challenges the spirit. Abandonment drives you into a state of shock, wondering why you have been rejected and erased from the lives of family and friends. To be abandoned is to walk through the world feeling invisible. To be abandoned is to sit in a room with family or friends and feel completely alone.

This is a dilemma victims of narcissistic abuse often face. We are isolated by our abusers. Then, the influence of the abusers convinces others to turn away. We are blamed. We are doubted. We are disbelieved. We are abandoned. The more we try to explain, the more distant family and friends become. The victim is left to survive in a vast world of emptiness and despair.

Victims of narcissistic abuse are often punished twice. First, we are isolated by our abuser, cut off from friendships, discouraged from reaching out, and silenced by control. Then the abuser spreads their poison, turning family, friends, even our own children against us.

I have been cut off from my grandchildren. I was isolated from the innocent love I once believed would be my legacy. I was driven away from the peace I found in places like the Qigong group on Hilton Head Island. The man I married stripped me of anything that gave me joy. His goal was clear: **isolate me, control me, erase me.**

Isolation is not quiet. It is a loud, suffocating stillness. It is life lived in the shadows, unseen, unheard, unloved. I was isolated and abandoned, but I am still here. They erased me from their lives, but they did not erase my voice. They isolated me, but in that isolation, I found a mirror. In that mirror, I viewed a new version of me. The version who no longer fears to speak her truth.

Existential Loneliness

Existential loneliness is a feeling of disconnection, separation, fear, anguish, and loss of purpose in life. I experienced existential loneliness every day for the past two years and counting. I feel erased, unclaimed, unloved, abandoned, and discarded by the family I love. I do not matter. My voice is not heard. My truth is silenced. I go through the motions of living, but I am starving from the lack of respect, kindness, and acknowledgement from the people I love. I breathe, but I do not feel alive. Existential loneliness is not about needing other people. It is about needing to matter to someone, needing to be loved and valued, needing to be recognized and appreciated as a human being.

So often I wonder: Does anyone know I exist? Does anyone care? "I am submerged in the deepness of existential loneliness. Will I ever be rescued?"

No One Cared That I Vanished

I disappeared slowly. Not all at once. Not with screams or broken glass. Just a quiet unraveling. A little less laughter. A little more silence. A dimming light in my eyes that no one noticed. The man I married watched it happen and called it peace. My son saw it and called me unstable. Friends faded as if grief were contagious.

I stopped talking. Stopped reaching. Stopped hoping. No one asked why. No one came looking. No one cared that I vanished. But I did. I saw the woman disappearing. I heard her silence. I felt her fading.

I gathered my warrior's strength. I came back, not with joy but with truth, and to say, I am here; I exist; I matter.

To the woman who is vanishing quietly: I see you. I hear you. I am you. You are not alone.

When Hope Was Gone

There was a time, just a few months ago, when I could not see a future. The truth had finally come into focus. The man I married had taken off the mask. I saw clearly what had always been there: control, deception, emptiness. Friends and family had abandoned me. The world looked different after that. I felt stripped down, hollowed out. I had nothing left to give, not even to myself.

Thoughts of my grandchildren kept me here. I thought, *"Let me hold on long enough to secure something for them."* That thought gave me strength and a reason for my existence.

I was experiencing a constant kind of internal mental and physical pain that I did not know the body could endure. I thought about ending it all. Not as an act of desperation, but as a final release from the quiet torment I was living with for far too long.

I write this with pure honesty and certainly not for pity. I write it because others need to know the truth: narcissistic abuse does not just hurt; it erodes the will to live. If you have been there, you are not alone. You are human, you are strong, and you are still here just like me.

Grief

Grief is the experience of coping with loss. It is not just an emotion; it is a powerful, overwhelming force. Grief lives in the body. It is the hollow ache in the pit of the stomach. It is the tightness in the chest. It is the heaviness in the bones. It is exhaustion that has no name. Grief is the quiet, invisible wound that follows narcissistic abuse.

The Stages of Grief as described by Dr. Elisabeth Kübler-Ross:

- *Denial*
- *Anger*
- *Bargaining*
- *Depression*
- *Acceptance*

The stages are not linear. Survivors of abuse often move back and forth between them, stuck in one stage for months or skipping another entirely. I feel as if the stage of acceptance is a distant shore that I might never reach.

Grief is ever-present in my life. I grieve so many things: The life I thought I had. The family I believed in. The love that was never real.

Grief overwhelms me. It is triggered by everyday moments. I see a picture. I hear a song. I watch a movie. I see a couple walking down the street. I pass a family gathered in a park. A memory flashes, and I am undone. I feel weak. I feel sick. I feel sad. I feel grief.

I have a wonderful counselor. I meet with her weekly. She is helping me deal with my grief issues. She is one of my Earth angels. She listens. She believes me. She understands the hidden damage caused by narcissistic abuse. She works with people who carry invisible wounds. She helps me carry mine. I am deeply grateful for her and for the domestic violence organization that made this healing connection possible.

Hurdles

There are many hurdles that challenge victims of narcissistic abuse on the journey to healing. There is cognitive dissonance when the abuse is clear, yet memories of the good moments distort reality and create confusion. There is emotional attachment, a sense of connection and affection toward another person, often aligned with dependence.

There is silence, the choice to stop revealing personal details, to limit conversations, and to keep interactions short and purposeful.

Overcoming these hurdles takes strength, discipline, and unwavering willpower. But with practice, each step forward becomes an act of reclaiming yourself.

Cognitive Dissonance

Cognitive dissonance is a psychological phenomenon that occurs when a person holds two conflicting or contradictory beliefs simultaneously. Cognitive dissonance is a challenging hurdle to overcome. It is a constant struggle that emits negative side effects along the journey to healing and recovery from narcissistic abuse.

I have memories of times when I thought the man I married was my loving and devoted husband. We shared special moments, special engagements, and special events. Moments when I thought we experienced happiness. These were the moments I perceived as love, trust, and loyalty. Memories that are locked away in my conscious mind of a time that was. The man I married removed his mask and revealed a version of himself that is unrecognizable. The version of him that is not loving, not kind, not honest, and not loyal. Now, this stranger I live with vacillates between the two versions of himself. This vacillation confuses the conscious mind. The mind wants to believe the good version still exists, but the bad version is there in plain sight; it cannot be denied. Victims of abuse must be cognizant of cognitive dissonance.

Emotional Attachment

Emotional attachment is a deep bond that connects you to another person. Your happiness is often centered around another person. It becomes unhealthy when you look to another for emotional support and there is no reciprocity. This is a trap for victims of narcissistic abuse. This attachment is formed over time in a narcissistic relationship. The victim longs for approval and love from the abuser. The victim becomes dependent upon the narcissist. Emotional attachment is a great hurdle to overcome in healing from narcissistic abuse.

Emotional detachment can be a coping mechanism for the victim of narcissistic abuse. Emotional detachment from a narcissist is not an easy venture.

However, it can be a potent advancement on the journey to healing and recovery. The victim relinquishes the emotions that keep one tethered to the narcissist. That entails limiting terms of support, adulation, admiration, engagement, interaction, and communication with the narcissist. You must be diligent and consistent.

PRACTICES OF DETACHMENT

— *Prioritize yourself*

— *Set boundaries*

— *Keep silent*

— *Keep records*

— *Save money*

— *Seek therapy*

— *Plan an escape*

— *Engage in meditation*

— *Accept what you can not fix*

I am slowly and definitively incorporating the practices of emotional detachment. In the past, when I grocery shopped, I always purchased items that the man I married wanted. Today, I prioritize myself. I purchase the items I want. I have had a separate bank account for the first time since being married to this man. I remain calm when confronted with any engagement with this man and his attempts to bait me. I simply walk away seemingly unbothered.

Silence

My niece recently shared a memory she recalled from long ago. She said she remembers a time when her grandmother, my mother, told her that I tell the man I married everything. She said a woman should never tell a man everything.

My niece sharing that memory was a powerful awakening. There were so many red flags I missed during the early years of my relationship with this man, I married.

 I was always naively transparent about everything. He was my trusted confidant to whom I revealed my strengths and my weaknesses. I did not realize I was providing him with weapons and ammunition that would be used to devastate and destroy me.

I have learned it is not wise to share too much information with the narcissist. Minimize the conversation; share only what is absolutely necessary.

Make responses short; do not elaborate.

When one shouts, screams, or demands to be recognized or heard, it fuels the narcissist. It provides the energy that fuels their ego. They maintain power and control. Stay calm in the storm. It is not easy; it takes practice and resilience to remain calm and silent. Silence is a powerful weapon to use in the warfare against narcissistic abuse. Silence is my weapon of choice. Silence speaks volumes!

Revelation

Over the past two years, I felt disoriented and displaced in this world without the persona of the man I thought I married. I had been conditioned and controlled by him for so long. It is a struggle of survival to live in this house with a stranger; a man I do not know. We merely exist in the same time and space; there is no connection.

I mistakenly sought relief from external forces far too long during the past two years. I wanted someone to fix me; I wanted someone to stop the pain; I wanted someone to rescue me. I had visions of the man I thought I knew for 51 years. I desperately needed him. I cried for him; I longed for him; I grieved for him. I was shaken to my core, weak and broken. I was lost in a state of pain, confusion, and loneliness.

There I was, crying out again in vain. No one was coming to save me. It was like the days with my maternal grandmother when I cried for a mother who never came. This time, I cried for the man I married. The stranger who dwelled with me had no interest in saving me; his objective was the devastation and destruction of me. My expiration date with him had been circled on the calendar with a permanent marker.

In my deep sorrow, I cried to friends and family. Some people listened, offered support, and empathized. Others turned their backs on me, believing the man I married to be the stable one in the marriage.

They assumed something was wrong with me. They assumed that I had deficits, was flawed, was unstable, and that I needed mental help. I relinquished contact with people who displayed doubts about my stability.

It was an excruciatingly painful venture to write this book. There are so many painful memories. The experience brought forth so much clarity as to what happened to me. I cried many days as I worked on this manuscript. The experience triggered so much grief. Before I decided to write, I thought I was healing. There is no healing from what the man I married put me through for 54 years. This will be a lifetime of pain that will end when I die. The depth of pain is too deep; recovery is not possible for me.

One day, a moment of revelation descended like a quiet truth. I had been seeking help in all the wrong places. I was reaching outwardly. I was desperate for answers, clinging to external voices when what I truly needed was to turn inward. My healing had to begin within me. So I began to pray daily and intentionally for guidance, for protection, for peace. I surrounded myself with healing meditations, letting their words fill the silence of my days and nights. I started walking, setting a goal of 10,000 steps each day. Each step became its own kind of therapy. The rhythm of my feet on the pavement felt like a slow reclaiming of self. I dusted off the Nordic track bike, once forgotten, and began again, starting at resistance level one and slowly climbing to level eight. What had once collected dust now became a symbol of determination. Something awakened in me. The warrior within began to rise, and from that place of stillness and strength, I began a forceful fight for survival.

I have come to accept that the man I married exhibits patterns and behaviors that align with what I now understand to be narcissistic abuse. I want to be clear: I am not a mental health professional, and I do not claim to diagnose anyone. What I share comes from years of lived experience, personal research, and the painful process of recognizing repeated emotional harm that I once had no name for.

He is who he is. I no longer expect change, and yet, I hold space for empathy. I know this was likely not the life he would have chosen for himself either. In many ways, he is also a product of his upbringing, of painful life experiences, and inherited emotional patterns.

And still, I grieve. I grieve the life we could have had. I grieve the moments we lost to dysfunction and distortion. I grieve for both of us and for the love that was never safe enough to grow and could not be kept alive.

If you are reading this and feel even the faintest whisper that you may be living in a narcissistic relationship, please do not silence that voice. Educate yourself. Learn what narcissistic abuse really looks like and how it hides in plain sight. Seek out people who will hear you, believe you, and walk beside you without judgment. Do not let your life unravel in silence, the way mine nearly did. You

are worthy of truth, of peace, and of reclaiming what remains of yourself.

Do not let your destination be devastation and destruction.

I end with the words of Maya Angelou:

"A wise woman wishes to be no one's enemy; a wise woman refuses to be anyone's victim."

I am on a journey. My destination: To become a wise woman.

Carl Jung Quotes

Carl Jung was a Swiss psychiatrist and one of the founding voices in modern psychology. His work on the unconscious mind, identity, and the human shadow has helped shape how we understand both personality and trauma.

Many of his insights speak deeply to the inner experiences of narcissists and the silent suffering of their victims. The quotes below have given me clarity, strength, and moments of deep reflection. I share them with the hope that they will speak to you, too.

"Who looks outside, dreams; who looks inside, awakes."

"You are what you do, not what you say you'll do."

"In each of us, there is another whom we do not know."

"The privilege of a lifetime is to become who you truly are."

"We don't get wounded alone, and we don't heal alone."

"We don't heal anything; we just let go."

"Shame is a soul-eating emotion."

"Embrace your grief, for there your soul will grow."

These words remind me that healing is not about becoming someone new, it is about reclaiming who I always was.

Final Thoughts

A time came when reality beamed brightly and clearly. It shocked my nervous system. It rocked my world. I had educated myself. I had learned. I had observed. I knew; I just knew; I was living in a narcissistic, abusive relationship. There was no slight deniability. There was illuminating clarity.

A person I loved; a person I trusted; a person I married, manipulates me, controls me, betrays me, and deceives me on a continuum. The marriage I thought was real and genuine was a mere illusion of happiness, loyalty, respect, love, sincerity, kindness, devotion, and family. I was deceived to believe it was authentic for 51 years before I awoke to reality.

When you are in a narcissistic relationship, none of what is believed to be true is real. It is an orchestrated performance by a master conductor. The star performer receives accolades and adulations from devoted admirers. These admirers constantly seek some form of validation from the star performer: a word, a gesture, a kindness, or a recognition. Anything the star performer directs keeps the admirers enchanted and mesmerized.

I have clarity. I have understanding. The person the public sees is charming, charismatic, generous, and kind. The narcissist is the deceptive person who remains hidden behind the mask. The narcissist only unmasks in the presence of targeted victims. Victims are the only ones who see the person who lurks behind the mask.

The narcissist's actions, thoughts, and behaviors are quite different from the norm. They justify in their minds all the harm, the damage, and the pain they inflict on others. They lie, they cheat, and they steal because they are "entitled," they are "exceptional," they are "special." There is not any thing or anyone that can change the narcissist. When you understand this truth and accept what it is, you are on a pathway to healing.

I have lived with the man I married for almost 54 years, now. I feel that I have wasted the one life one gets on this Earth, loving a person who is not capable of loving me. I sacrificed my life, unknowingly, to live in a delusional world created by a narcissist. I loved him, but he never loved me. Experts on narcissism say the way a narcissists treats you is not about you, it is about them. Perhaps they are right. However, I feel the abuse I endured from the man I married was issued on me on a personal level. I believe I was the one person on Earth that he hated the most. I will never understand why.

I hope my story resonates with people who suspect they are living in the nightmare of a narcissistic relationship. Save yourself. Save your children. Save your family. Educate yourself; know whom and what you are dealing with.

The man I met and married over five decades ago is a person I did not know then, and I do not know him now. He wore an appealing mask of deception. He successfully charmed his way into my life. I admit, I wanted him in my life. I thought he was the man of my dreams, a true soulmate; I was wrong. Lurking behind the mask was the man of my nightmares. The man I married devastated and destroyed my soul. There is no recovery for me.

Advocate For Victims Of Narcissist Abuse

There is a dangerous gap in understanding among many therapists, doctors, and mental health professionals when it comes to narcissistic abuse.

Too often, victims are misdiagnosed, misunderstood, or dismissed. When a narcissistic abuser presents themselves as calm, concerned, rational, and the victim shows signs of distress, confusion, or fear, the professional may side with the wrong person. The abuser is believed. The victim is labeled. I know this because it happened to me.

I have had sessions with psychiatrists and therapists where I told my truth about the man I married. I spoke about the emotional abuse, the fear, the erasure of my identity.

They saw only a distressed woman. When the abuser spoke next, his performance was calm and flawless. The result? No acknowledgment of the abuse. No validation of my suffering.

Just a vague suggestion that we "have a communication problem" or "go our separate ways." No one called it abuse. No one saw the danger I was still in. I was left feeling invisible and devastated.

This has to change.

Professionals should be educated on the reality of narcissistic personality disorder and covert abuse. They must understand that the calmest person in the room is not always the safest.

That victims often present as anxious, reactive, or broken because they have been shattered from the inside out. Victims are left to feel hopeless and helpless. My experience with mental health professionals exacerbated my feelings of devastation and destruction.

Addendum: A Day Of Messages

Four Messages. One Day.

June 22, 2025

This was not an easy decision. I debated whether to include these messages between my son and me. They are painful and deeply personal, but the truth deserves light.

I have redacted names out of respect for privacy. My intention is not to cause harm or to shame any human being. It is simply to share honestly the emotional toll of a relationship that has been marked by silence, rejection, and unspoken grief.

These exchanges reveal more than just words. They reveal the patterns, the wounds, and the pain of not being believed, of being called unstable, and of watching a child mirror the emotional cruelty of his father.

These four messages were exchanged between my son and me on a single day. I share them now, not to shame or retaliate, but to reveal the emotional toll of a relationship shaped by deep pain, blame, and denial. My words came from a place of reflection, endurance, and truth. His words came from a place I still struggle to understand. May this speak to those who have lived in silence.

I have loved my son deeply. I still do, but I will not silence my story to make others more comfortable. This is not about vengeance. It is about giving voice to what was endured in silence for far too long. This is my truth. This is what survival looks like.

Dear son,

I came to you yesterday not in weakness, but in courage. I came as a mother who has endured more than you will ever fully understand. I came hoping for the smallest gesture of humanity. Instead, I was met with coldness, blame, and silence.

You read my letters, then dismissed them without a word. You spoke not from compassion, but from accusation. And when I asked for a simple hug, not out of pity, but out of love, you turned your back and walked away.

That moment broke something in me, but not my dignity. What it shattered was the illusion that there was still warmth left in you for the woman who brought you into this world.

You may justify your actions. You may convince yourself that I deserved it. But one day, if you have the courage to look honestly at your reflection, you will remember this day, and how you treated your own mother when she stood before you with nothing but open hands and open heart.

I loved you. I protected you. I suffered in silence to give you stability. I stayed in a broken home, not because I was weak, but because I was trying to hold together the pieces of a life torn apart by cruelty and manipulation. You saw only parts of it, but you never saw me.

I will not apologize for speaking my truth. I will not hide the pain I feel. I will no longer chase after scraps of affection from a son who treats me as if I no longer matter.

This letter is not a plea. It is a declaration. I exist. I love. I endure. I deserve more than what you gave me.

You may never look back. But you cannot erase the truth of who I am, the mother who loved, nurtured, and raised you. You cannot deny that for a few moments you had to read the words of a mother you chose to forget.

I will move forward now—not because you gave me closure, but because I gave it to myself.

Your mother,

Veronica

My Son's Revealing Message:

Just to let you know…You were a decent mother. I understand that you did the best you could do, with what you had. Despite all of the trauma you claim, you both did a decent job raising me. I worked hard for over 30 years. Still raising 6 kids. Still growing as a person. I love you and will always love you.

Your recent behavior is alarming. I'm not a doctor, but I do believe you suffer from some sort of dementia. Your behavior is similar to [Aunt #1] when she came here. It's also similar to my aunt [Aunt #2]'s behavior. I've advocated and will continue to advocate for you to receive the proper treatment for all of your afflictions.

There are things that have festered between us that have created hard feelings. Example…When I was married to (person's name), you stated early on that she wasn't nurturing or motherly. You'd constantly take shots at her. I defended her. You'd get upset at me defending "MY WIFE, MY WIFE!" You completely twisted that point in your book by stating it was me who complained about her. You complained. No accountability from you. Any retractions? Doubt it. You also harped on how (person's name), her mother, and her sisters isolated you when we had gatherings together. Also, you were the first person who stated, "It would be ok if you divorced." I guess you let bygones be bygones. I reconnected with (person's name), and you brought her in the garage to give her a 2 hour info session about me. The things you talked about get used as ammunition to this day. Thanks Mom! Incidentally you did the same thing with (person's name). It was all good until she blurted out in court that I was an alcoholic and you were a manic depressive. There's your ammunition right back at you. It's almost as if you try to sabotage me. What's insane is that now you don't speak to (person's name) and can't explain why. You were buddy-buddy, and then it turned off. Discarded in true form. Just like (person's name), who you're now buddy-buddy. That's odd. Trying to dig at me and (person's name) by saying how pretty (person's name) looks now or how happy she seems now. You're pretty low for that pettiness. I'm happy for (person's name) and her success. Her success is good for my sons. We've had a decent enough relationship as coparents of our children. You also seem to have forgotten how she was with (child's name). So bad that you and (friend's name) had to leave as we were moving into our house in (a town), and also in case you forgot, (person's name)was not employed. She was an alcoholic. She didn't take the boys to practice and games. She and her parents didn't respect my sleep time so that I could go to work. You claimed, "Those people are trying to kill you!" I guess you didn't want to include that context in your book. Now you throw it in my face to say how pretty she is and how happy she looks. Great job, MOM.

Now that I'm married to(person's name) you inexplicably stopped talking to her AND HER MOTHER… Her mother?? What did she do to you?? Not a damn thing!! That's an illness. I understand that and implore you to get help.

I also have more issues with your book. I tried to kill myself twice when I was a teenager. It was not because of what I feared my father would do to me. It was because I felt that I failed you. I failed to meet your expectations. And I felt like I couldn't win. I went to school and lacked organization skills. I lacked certain disciplines to stay focused. I'm not sure I could overcome those things then. So I would get very upset at your reactions to my issues in school. Had nothing to do with him. With all that said, I didn't consent to personal information like that going in your book. WHAT MOTHER DOES THAT?!? The day you kicked me out of your house, you stated very clearly that you were going to put me in your memoir. Almost like, you were getting vengeance on me for daring to disagree with you. That's narcissism. Projection much?? Well, I guess you got me back. Thanks again, MOM.

In those papers you gave me yesterday, you asked, "Where was your heart when I needed my son the most? Where was your voice when I had none left?" You state that my father is some abusive monster, but you allowed him to drunk drive your 7 year old around town until the wee hours of the morning. He'd be so drunk that I often had to steer the car to keep us alive and on the road. I told you that, back then. You allowed this shitty little girl at (school name) to call me NIGGER every day. I told you that, when it happened. These things happened on your watch too. You allowed (woman's name) to treat me any kind of way. I hated her!! (cousin's name) used to bully me and beat me up. Clearly, my father should take the hit on this stuff, too. I'd come home with black eyes and busted lips. You desperately want to be the victim. Ask yourself, where was my mother when these things happened? It's crazy to think that my mother lumps me in with my father, who she claims abuses her.

Sorry to vent or retort in such long form, as some would put it. I'm not going to allow you to paint the narrative on me. I love you. I know you need help and clearly aren't getting it. Eventually, you won't be able to mask it for those strangers who listen to your troubles, and as you say, "they believe me!" The people who know you, see that you need help. They don't believe you. I wish you would take the advice from those who know you best, as opposed to strangers.

PS:

I think it's dangerous for you to drive. I don't think you are capable anymore of driving. If you were to crash and hurt somebody's child, it would be devastating. Please consider that. I love you. I hope you get some help.

MY RESPONSE:

Thank you for writing to me. I read every word carefully, and I can hear that you are carrying much pain. You've expressed your truth, and while some of it is painful to receive, I honor your need to say it.

You are my son; I will always love you. That will never change. I never set out to harm you, not as a mother and not as a writer. I wrote my book to make sense of my life, to find healing after years of enduring in silence. I finally spoke my truth. For decades, I was used, abused, and deceived by someone I thought loved me. It was never written against you, but for my own survival. It pains me that you interpret it that way.

I know I wasn't perfect; I know I made major mistakes. I'm sorry for the ways I may have failed you. But I always tried to love and to protect you, even when I was fighting to protect myself. We both needed protection. This is my truth.

I'm also aware of the concerns you've expressed about my mental capacity and ability to function. I want to reassure you, gently but clearly, that I remain fully capable mentally, emotionally, and physically. I've spent the past two years working as a substitute teacher, primarily with high school students. I was asked to come work at RCHS. I got up every school day at 5:30 for five months, December to May and drove myself to work. I developed lesson plans and graded papers for students at the 9th and 10th grade levels. I have continued to engage with life thoughtfully and responsibly.

I know who I am. I know what I've lived through. I know the difference between truth and distortion. If peace between us is ever to be possible, it will need to be rooted in mutual respect where both of our truths are honored, without attempting to erase the other. I remain open to that, if and when it becomes possible.

With love,

Your mother,

Veronica

My Son's Second Message Of Revelations

"I believe in THE TRUTH. Not mine. Not yours. There are things in our intertwined lives that definitely happened. Not your truth or mine. They happened, and we both observed them. When I disagreed with you and you threw me out of your house, that definitely happened. Not your truth, not mine. It's just the truth. As you were shouting at me, you stated loud and clear, "I'm writing about you in my memoir!!" Not your truth or mine. Just the truth. That sounded very much like an intent to hurt me. The pages upon pages where you tell readers that your child was abusive toward you, sound like viscous intent. You tried to destroy me.

When you tell (person's name) how pretty she is and hug her after spurning me at Stevie's senior night, how is that not an intentional attempt at hurting me. Can you tell me what we (me, my wife and mother in law) did to deserve the wrath of "YOUR" truth We definitely see the optics and the things you've done. That's not my truth. That's THE truth. Can you be specific and give me some explanation of why this happened?

When you say, peace between us comes through mutual respect, where's the respect for me. You just glossed over everything you say you read. I'd like your answers to the questions I've posed. I'd like specific replies to the things I mentioned. How did it completely flip from one extreme with (person's name)to the other. Same with (person's name). I'd like to know how you, in good conscience, avoid acknowledging that you intended harm with your book. "My son and his girlfriend…" That part sounded intentional. I'd love an explanation for these things?

Anyone who intentionally distorts "THEIR" truth should let the correction be as loud and boisterous as the distortion. The fact that you work in the school system does not change the behaviors I have directly witnessed for years. It's not just me, apparently. You screenshotted texts from your mutual friends in HHI. They are concerned too. You took those texts as a threat when there was no threatening language in the texts. Please point out where the lady threatened you. If you are ok, then let's all go to a doctor and make sure. Shouldn't be any problem with that. When WE go to a doctor and a doctor clears you, I will be convinced. If you are just fine, nothing to worry about. We'll all be relieved. If you're not ok, then we will have identified something and get you the proper care. We do this because we care for you. Let me know when we can go see a doctor together.

I've already acknowledged the things that happened in my life. I've given you specifics. Nowhere are you specific. Answer some hard questions. Then maybe it will look like mutual respect from your end."

My Response

My response was no response. I decided not to respond to my son's second message. The exchange was going nowhere. His words were sharp, unwavering, and fixed on a version of me I no longer recognized. I sensed that nothing I said could change his mind, so I stayed silent.

The Next Morning

The next morning, my son called his father. I did not hear the conversation, but the man I married shared a brief account of it with me. He said our son told him they needed to proceed with the plan they had once discussed, seeking a court order to have me evaluated and possibly committed. According to him, he told our son he had no inclination to pursue such a venture. That was the end of it, at least from what he shared.

This plan is not new. It was born some time ago, sparked by a scathing "diagnosis" made by Martha Pike, a woman who once knew me casually. We were friendly at one time on Hilton Head Island, SC. I had not spoken to her or seen her in years. Her judgment did not come from any recent experience or any direct observation, but from a story told to her by the man I married. That story was enough for her to write a scathing diagnosis that I was seriously mentally ill and needed to be committed to an institution.

The two people I love, who claim to care for me, could so easily revisit the idea of silencing me legally and medically, which deepens my pain. That is a betrayal that words can barely hold. It is not a concern. It is control, and because they cannot shape my truth, they want to dismiss it. "I will not be silent," I speak my truth.

Awareness After The Storm

I wrote about the pain I endured, the cruelty, the silence, and the rejection. I wrote about my maternal grandmother, the man I married, and the son who no longer sees me as his mother. I saw myself as a victim who was controlled, silenced, manipulated, deceived, and abandoned by the man I married, the man who wears a mask of charm, and a son who mirrors his father. Their actions cause me deep wounds and invisible scars.

After reading the exchange of messages between my son and me, I began to see something I had not been ready to face, something about me, something about my failures. As I near the end of this book, I realize there is more truth that needs to be told. It is not a reversal of what I said. It is an act of ownership. I made many mistakes in my life.

As my son was growing and developing, I tried to shape him into who I thought he needed to be. I wanted him to be well-behaved, smart, and a "little preppy type."

I wanted to prepare him for the world stage. I wanted him to be a bright light that illuminated the world. He was to become a reflection of the mother who proudly raised him. I did not allow him to be his own person. I encouraged him to be someone I envisioned. I never consider his visions for himself. My control, expressed as love and protection, wounded my son. I take full ownership of that.

I was not the only one harmed in the story I tell. In telling the truth about what was done to me, I must also tell the truth about what I failed to see and what I failed to protect. Truth means acknowledging that I contributed to the breakdown in my relationship with my son. I did not create all the pain, but I was not blameless. There are choices I made, silences I kept, and signs I missed, especially when he was young and needed more from me than I could give.

Now, I live with a sorrow that has no remedy and regrets that cannot be undone. I mourn the mother I was not. I did not recognize the damage when it mattered most, when he was still reachable. I recognize it now, but it feels too late. That is a grief I carry every day.

"It takes courage to face the truth, not only about others, but about yourself."

Reflections in the Garage

I am sitting alone in the garage, reflecting on past events in my life. In the stillness of this quiet space, something rises in me, something I can no longer keep buried. I am stunned. Stunned by the magnitude of what this man did to me. For decades, I had no idea. No idea what I was enduring.

No idea that the pain I carried was not because I was broken, but because I had been broken down slowly, silently, strategically. I lived with a gnawing ache, a quiet voice in the back of my mind that whispered, "You are not enough." I carried that voice long before I ever met the man I married. It did not begin with him. That voice was born in childhood. I reflect on growing up under the roof of my grandmother, a strong, proud woman who had survived her own storms. She kept the family together. She was a force of nature. She was not soft. She was not loving. She did not believe in comfort. Emotions were not to be shown.

Weakness was not allowed. In her world, survival came through control. There was food on the table, structure in the home, but there was no emotional shelter. No space to feel afraid. No room to say, "I need help." So I did not say it. I learned how to be quiet; how to be pleasing; how to be useful.

When I married, I stepped right into the same familiar pattern, a life of emotional abandonment disguised as stability. The man I married did not need to scream. He erased me in other ways. He erased me with his silence; with his contempt; with his hatred; with his deception. He erased me with the kind of neglect that looks calm from the outside, but destroys you on the inside. I gave him everything: my love, my money, my time, my youth, my loyalty. I asked for so little in return. I just wanted to be loved. I just wanted to be safe. That was asking far too much from him. So I shrank. I bent myself trying to become the kind of woman he could finally treat with kindness.

I am awakening, but I still live with the struggles and pain that greet me each day. The man I married pretends to be kind to me these days as we prepare for our move back to Hilton Head Island. I cannot unsee the truth, the contempt, and hatred he carries in his heart for me, the woman who has always truly loved him. I now understand who he truly is. Yet, I will probably always love the version of him I thought I knew. That person, the man I believed in, will live inside of me forever.

Even after you see the truth, you may still love the version of them you thought was real. That love was built on moments carefully designed to bond you. The moments your heart still remembers, even when your mind knows better. It is not a weakness to feel that love linger. It means you are human and you are grieving someone who never truly existed. You are not loving the abuser standing in front of you, you are loving a ghost. A part of healing is letting the ghost rest.

Today, at seventy-eight years old, I finally accept the truth:

It was never me. It was always him.

He saw my cracks and used them to build his power.

He exploited my silence, my shame, and my need to be good.

I survived. Today, in this garage, I breathe in the truth:

I am not weak.

I am not inferior.

I am not invisible.

I am as good as any other human.

Yes, here it is, another day that I sit alone in the garage, my place of peace, reflection, tears, and prayer. I tell myself I have finished writing my book, but more thoughts rise to the surface. My book may be complete, but my story has not ended.

Survival Spaces

Sometimes survival is quiet.

It is sitting in the garage.

It is locking the bathroom door just to cry.

It is getting into the back seat of your car in a Walmart parking lot because you cannot break down at home.

These are not signs of weakness, they are signs of strength.

They are the spaces we retreat to when the house becomes a stage, and pretending becomes too heavy to bear.

If you are reading this as you sit in your own kind of garage, feeling invisible, reflecting on your pain, feeling the slow erasure of your spirit, you are not alone. There are others like you who are abused and betrayed by the people they love and trust. We must believe in ourselves and love ourselves. We are not crazy; we are not weak; we are survivors, warriors. Our lives matter.

A Final Plea from a Victim of Narcissistic Abuse

"PLEASE MAKE THEM STOP HURTING ME!"

"I breathe, but I do not feel alive."

I exist, but I am not seen.
I speak, but I am not heard.
I cry, but my tears go unnoticed.
I ache, but no one asks why.
This is not living.
This is surviving in a body that remembers everything.

They say, "He is a good man."
They do not see the silence that slices like a knife.
They do not see the smiles that hide the control.
They do not see the soul of a woman slowly dying.

I scream, but only on the inside.
I beg, but only with my eyes.
I wake up each day in a prison no one else can see.
It is a prison of manipulation, gaslighting, and quiet destruction.
I was a woman with dreams and light in her eyes.
Now I am a shadow, begging for mercy.

Please make them stop hurting me.
Please believe me.
Please see me. Please hear me.

I exist.

Message To Victims Of Narcissistic Abuse

By Veronica Harvin

RELEASE WHAT WAS

Let go of what you hoped it was.

It was never love. It was never safety.

Release the lies you believed.

Release the illusion so you can see the truth.

There is a pattern. It is happening every day, in every town, across every race and social class: a woman lives in quiet terror beside a man who drains her soul, confuses her mind, and punishes her for daring to feel, speak, or exist.

He may never hit her, but he hits her spirit with shame, silence, and subtle destruction.

He rewrites the truth until she doubts her own name. She becomes a stranger to herself.

When she finally breaks or tries to break free, he either destroys her or convinces the world she destroyed herself. These stories show up in the news as domestic disputes, mental illness, or tragic suicides.

Rarely do we hear the real words: **narcissistic abuse**.

No one says it, but I will.

ACCEPT WHAT IS

The truth may be devastating, but it will set you free.

You may feel broken, but you are not beyond repair.

You may feel alone, but you are not the only one.

You are part of a silent army of survivors who are beginning to speak.

Narcissistic abuse is not just emotional abuse.

It is a system of psychological control designed to break you without bruises.

It makes you question your sanity, your worth, and your right to live.

If you are reading this and wondering if you are crazy, **you are not**.

If you are holding on by a thread, **you are not weak**. You are surviving what many will never understand.

MARCH FORWARD

Take back your voice. Reclaim your name.

Honor your story.

You do not owe your silence to anyone.

This book is not just my story. It is my witness. My battle cry.

I wrote it for women like you, women who are barely hanging on.

Please do not wait until it is too late.

Get safe. Get help. Get out.

You do not need proof to deserve protection.

You do not need permission to save your own life.

SURVIVE

Survive in the quiet. Survive in the chaos.

Survive when no one believes you.

Survive with dignity. Survive with grace.

Survive with truth.

You are not alone.

You were never crazy.

You are not invisible.

You are real. You are worthy.

If no one has told you today; know this, **"I believe you."**

Survive until you find your way out of the darkness and into the light.

When you do, **speak your truth.**

Covert Captivity

I live in a place that looks like freedom, but it is not. There are no locks on the doors. No chains around my wrists, I am not free. This is covert captivity. It is the kind of imprisonment that hides in plain sight. The world sees two older people sharing a home. What they do not see is the silence, the fear, the constant awareness that I am living with someone who once claimed to love me and now shows hatred for me.

There are no bruises to prove what I endure. There is only the steady erosion of safety and the quiet control. I speak kindly. I cook meals. I protect my own peace. I do not challenge him, not because I am weak, but because I am afraid of what he is capable of. His behavior is unpredictable. He needs supply; he is off balance. I know that his collapse could turn to cruelty in a moment.

Here I remain, struggling for survival inside a cage made of fear, history, and silence. Some women escape. Others, like me, remain behind bars, not because we choose captivity, but because we know what freedom might cost. This is my reality. This is where I live, at 78 years old, in captivity. If nothing changes, I will die in this captivity.

"Sometimes the cage is invisible, but the suffering inside it is real."

Waking Up In Old Age

Let my truth be your warning.

I am 78 years old.

And I just woke up.

I woke up to a truth I never wanted to see.

That was the life I built, the love I believed in, the man I trusted

were never real in the way I thought.

There is no peace here.

There is no safety.

There is no family to hold me.

Only the sharp clarity of betrayal and survival.

I gave him my youth.

I gave him my voice.

I gave him my love, my devotion, my decades.

I waited through silence, contempt, control, and isolation, believing

that one day it would all make sense.

It does now.

The truth did not bring healing.

It brought grief.

What I see at 78 is that I was never truly loved; I was only used.

My loyalty was manipulated.

My silence was rewarded with emptiness.

My needs were invisible.

I sit in this old body with young scars.

Scars from words that no one heard.

Scars from nights I cried myself to sleep in a house where I did not

feel safe.

Scars from being erased by the person I gave my life to.

And still—

I am here.

I see it now. I need you to see it too.

Do not let this happen to you.

Do not wait until you are 78 years old to realize your pain had a

name.

Do not spend a lifetime waiting to be treated like a human.

Do not give decades to someone who only wants your silence.

If you are reading this and you are still in it—consider getting out.

If you are doubting yourself—do not.

If you are the only one who sees the truth—believe yourself anyway.

You do not owe anyone your suffering.

You do not owe your silence to anyone.

You owe your life to **you.**

I am 78 years old. I am just now writing the truth.

Let that be your warning.

Let it also be your permission.

Sincerely,

Veronica Harvin